All the Sinners, Saints
Ron Jacobs

Fomite
Burlington, Vermont

ISBN-13: 978-1-937677-39-8
Library of Congress Control Number: 2012954599

Fomite
58 Peru Street
Burlington, VT 05401
www.fomitepress.com

Cover Design: Eric Gulliever

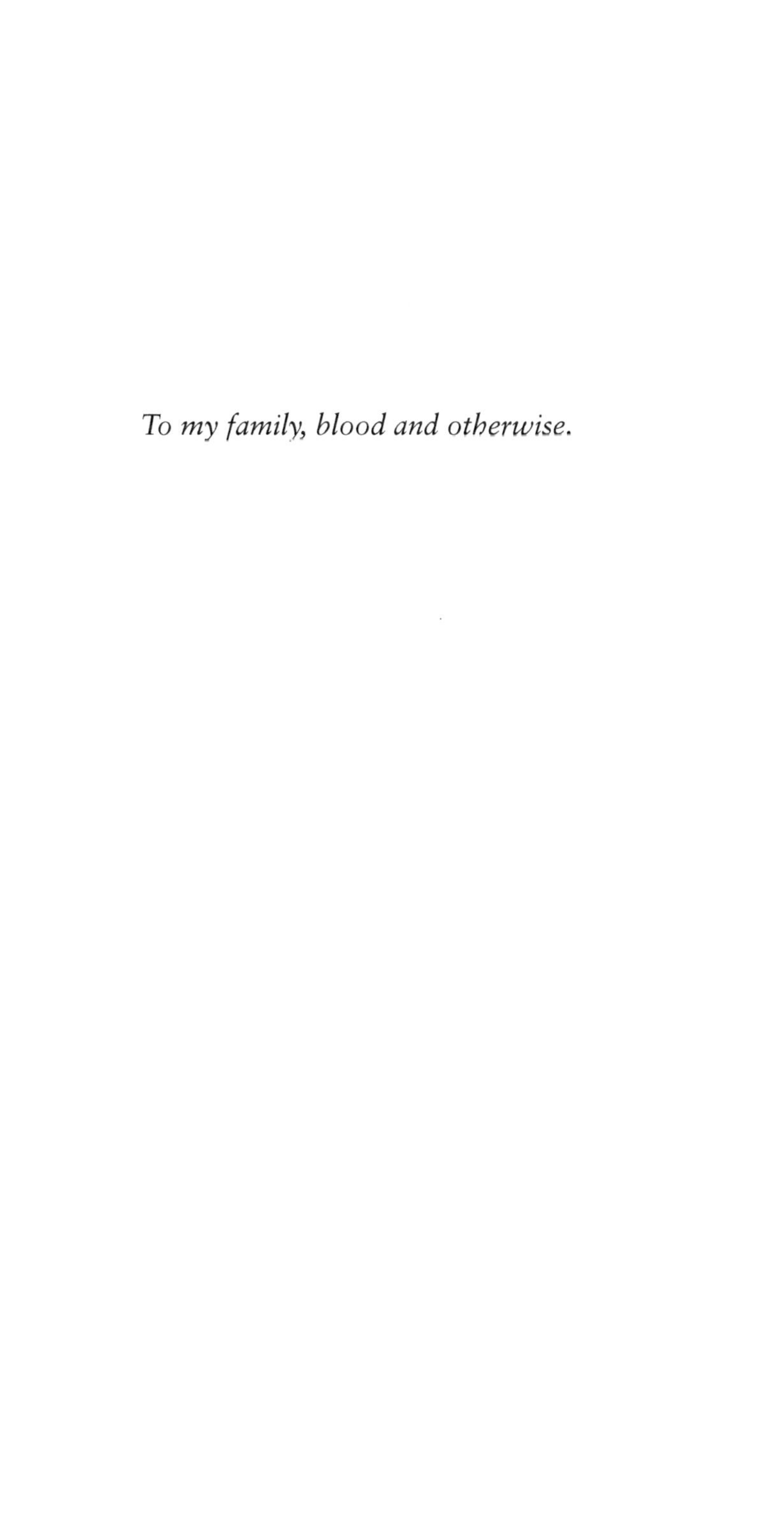

To my family, blood and otherwise.

Acknowledgements

As always, I am most grateful for the work of Fomite Press and its tremendous support. Without the efforts of Marc Estrin and Donna Bister, getting this novel to you would have been considerably more difficult and not nearly as much fun. The proofreading and editorial suggestions from Michael Day were spot on and crucial to the finished work. Of course and as always, the existence of my family and friends furthers my storytelling (a special thanks to Hannah!). Ian Thistle's suggestions regarding the opening essay "Crime Fiction and Capitalist Reality" were crucial to its lucidity. Plus, it was Ian who introduced me to cover artist Eric Gulliver, whose cover work is but a small part of his growing portfolio. In a backhanded way, I am grateful for the fact that my father was in the US military. If he had not been stationed in Frankfurt am Main during the period this novel is set in, I would not have partaken in nor observed the experiences that inspired me to create this story.

Abbreviations Used and Other Notes

AWOL-Absent Without Leave

CID- Criminal Investigation Division of the US Army CO-Commanding Officer

DKP-Deutsche Kommunisten Partei (German Communist Party)

FTA-Fuck the Army

GI- Government Issue-a tongue-in-cheek name for military member of low rank

MI- Military Intelligence

MP-Military Police

NCO-Non-Commissioned Officer

PX- Post Exchange

RAF-Rote Armee Fraktion (Red Army Faction)

SPD Socialistische Partei Demokratisch (Social Democratic Party)

This story takes place in Frankfurt am Main, Germany (Bundesrepublik Deutschland (BRD) when there were still two Germanys. Many Germans called Americans Amis, while many Americans called Germans Krauts. The foreign workers in Germany are called Gastarbeiter--literally guest workers. Most GIs lived on installations called Kasernes. Hashish was often called Scheiss or "shit." The visit of Fania Davis Jordan referred to in this story did occur. However, the actual date of the rally was a few weeks prior to the time period suggested here.

Crime Fiction and Capitalist Reality

The novel is generally acknowledged to be a bourgeois form of literature. It wasn't until there were enough literate people with time for leisurely reading that this entertainment came along. The crime novel reflects the bourgeois obsession with order and usually represents the concerns of that class. There is a crime against an individual that shakes up bourgeois society. A detective from the police force or a private investigator hunts down the perpetrator through a series of clues, makes the arrest and all is well again. Agatha Christie's novels are perfect examples of this. Then there are the tough guy novels featuring men like Mike Hammer. In this type of story, the protagonist easily forsakes the niceties of bourgeois society in his crime solving. Naturally, this alienates the police and the bourgeoisie, but he still gets the job done, captures (or kills) the criminal, and allows the middle class to get on with their lives. This representation is occasionally turned around and the protectors of order -- the police and courts -- are the criminals and by association so is the system they work for. This is noir.

Noir does not pretend that the society their protagonists operate in is worth saving. It's just the only one we have. This is where the novels of a few current writers exist, and where mine are intentionally placed. Writing about Italian noir for *World Literature Today* critic Madison J. Davis noted :

> The traditional mystery, deriving from Poe's "The Murders in the Rue Morgue" and evolving through Conan Doyle and Agatha Christie to contemporary practitioners like Carolyn G. Hart and Simon Brett, requires a certain faith in the legal system—or at least in a measure of justice parceled out to those who commit crimes. We live, however, in a skeptical world, in which even those who enjoy the puzzles and deductions of the traditional whodunit cannot see them as realistic. The events of the twentieth century have cracked, often splintered, our faith in the legal system and the triumph of justice, even in the good ole U. S. of A.

I would argue that the twenty-first century has brought us beyond even the skepticism Davis acknowledges. Indeed, skepticism seems almost quaint, when we read about hundreds of men being released from prison because they were jailed they for crimes they did not commit. Their incarceration was not due to a mistake, but a conscious decision by authorities to match a crime to the victim they chose. Every time news like this comes out, the credibility of the police as protectors of society diminishes. When working people see their friends and children going to prison for drug offenses while the wealthy usually avoid doing time, their perception of the legal system being rigged in favor of the wealthy and powerful is reinforced. Since the police are the most obvious representatives of that system (and the individuals most citizens encounter) they are no longer perceived as much more than enforcers of the rights of the wealthy and powerful. This perception, long held by those considered The Other in society, is now part of the common parlance. Indeed, television crime shows assume this in their portrayals of police departments and individual cops. Certain series, most notably David Simon's depressingly exquisite take on the corruption rampant in an entire city's political and legal system called *The Wire*, create a world where the incorruptible individual has no place.

This does not mean that the police don't enjoy at least tacit support by a majority of the population; it does mean that the number of people who believe the police are not above criminality is much diminished from just a few decades ago. The abuse of power by police during the protests of the 1960s and onwards; the revelations of individual cops like New York's Serpico regarding corruption and illegal arrests (among other things); the militarization of most police forces in cities and towns large and small; and the continued abrogation of civil liberties in the name of the war on drugs and the war on terrorism. All of these make the line between the police and the criminals they supposedly oppose very thin. Despite the multitude of cop shows on television attempting to present police as protectors of order and the innocent and even the presence of movies like Clint Eastwood's Dirty Harry series (which serve as propaganda for authoritarianism), many residents of modern society are convinced the police are not there for their sake.

Nor is the legal system. Occasionally a clever lawyer is able to keep an innocent person out of prison -- in real life and in fiction. Indeed, certain authors have made a good living writing legal thrillers that feature these kinds of stories. More often than not, however, the police and the courts conspire to convict the person in the docket no matter what. It's not that the conspiracy is intentional; it's just how the system works. Police arrest a person for a crime and the courts do the rest. Without a good attorney -- something very few can afford -- the suspect's options are very limited. If one adds a cop with a grudge, a judge with an agenda, or a politician with a law and order platform to the equation, that person in the docket does not stand a chance.

A few decades ago I was charged with "possession with the intent to sell" because I was sitting in an automobile when an acquaintance sold a small amount of marijuana to an undercover cop. This all went down not long after the state I was living in had passed a law that rendered the U.S. Constitution's prohibition on unreasonable search and seizure null and void. Anyone who was in the vicinity of anything having to do with illegal drugs was as culpable as the person actually involved with the drugs. So, since I was in the car when the drug deal occurred, I was also involved in the sale. When I showed up at court on the charge, I asked my public defender if I should challenge the charge and plead not guilty. His response was simple. If I challenged the charge I would not win. He advised me to take a plea deal and do community service. I took his advice. The law was not interested in justice, just in throwing people in jail.

Much anti-capitalist and antiwar activity is already labeled criminal in an imperial society. This in itself means that characters participating in activities that fall into this category are already suspect. Meanwhile, the forces of law and order trying to stifle such characters have a leeway not provided the citizen, no matter what he or she is involved in. The often violent reaction of the authorities to the Occupy Wall Street protests in Fall 2011 provides a recent example of this fact. A greater contradiction occurs when the forces of authority engage in criminal behavior in the pursuit of the forces aligned against the rulers the police are hired to protect. A further complication comes into play when criminal actions by the police are ignored or sanctioned while criminal acts by the targets of the authorities are not. In a line quite familiar to most rock and roll fans (especially those who listen to the Rolling Stones) that calls every cop a criminal, this contradiction is even clearer.

Back to that incorruptible individual. Most noir features a private investigator. Like the accused, he or she is an individual who lives on the edges of the law. In a world where the law itself can be unjust, only those not in debt to the system designed to bring justice can find that justice. Most often the investigator is one who works for hire with a set of morals that are immutable. In certain cases, like two of the novels in my 1970s trilogy, the investigators are regular folks determined to help a friend. Still, they are not without faults. Alcohol is often a vice these characters deal with. Most recently, in Thomas Pynchon's foray into the genre with a book titled *Inherent Vice,* his private eye smokes a lot of marijuana. Early on, many of the so-called tough guys like Mike Hammer were sexist and racist. As the genre has evolved, so have the investigators. Like the society they operate in, today's investigators include Blacks, Latinos, Asians, and women.

Today's noir fiction is the story of a system and society in decline. Marxist Ernest Mandel published a book on crime fiction in 1986 titled *Delightful Murder.* In this book, Mandel looks at the genesis and development of crime fiction. We see the development of the criminal from a lone individual whose exploits shock and dismay, but whom heroic police agents can capture. As capitalism moves into its monopoly phase, the lone criminal remains a problem, yet the real problem developing is an entire class of criminals. These are what Marx labeled the lumpenproletariat: that part of society whose sole task is surviving no matter what it takes. Usually extremely poor, only occasionally employed in conventional jobs, and existing literally outside of society, the lumpen are the truly dangerous ones in the bourgeoisie's midst. They provide respectable society with their entertainments such as illegal drugs and sex, but must be controlled at all cost. The investigator's position in society is closer to that of the lumpen than to any other stratum. He or she understands the justice of the streets is often not the justice of the courtroom. Of course, this position outside of society means there is nothing to lose in fighting the wealthy and powerful.

Mandel published his book before capitalism's latest phase was truly underway. That is, neoliberalism. This stage of monopoly capitalism is the nightmare that Rosa Luxembourg warned us about. Financiers who produce no product run the world. Instead of creating work, their actions profit from the destruction of jobs and the impoverishment of millions. They launder the millions made by international drug lords while financing politicians who want to build more prisons and lock up those who use the drugs. As far as the financiers are concerned, the working class itself is now a criminal class. Yet, we know better. It is the financiers and their class that are the true criminals. Still, they go free while workers go to jail for the crime of being poor. The conspiracy of the super rich is not an accident. They built the world that way.

Writers can choose to point this out or they can go along with the status quo. Good crime fiction on a neoliberal planet chooses the former. The task of those who write these tales is to point the finger at the true criminals. The police are only heroes when they bust the big guys. The system can only be just when it turns on its own. At this juncture in time, this only seems to happen in stories. Unfortunately.

Introductory Note

On August 7, 1970, 17-year-old revolutionary Jonathan Jackson (brother of Soledad Brother, Black Panther and author George Jackson), was attending the trial of the so-called Soledad Brothers in Northern California's Marin County courthouse. Without warning, he pulled a pistol from under his raincoat, ordering everyone to freeze. He then distributed guns from a briefcase to three of the Brothers who were on trial. The group moved outside toward an escape van rented by Jackson, taking five hostages, including Judge Harold Haley, an assistant district attorney and three female jurors. A sawed-off shotgun was taped under the chin of the judge. His plan was to get to an airport, hijack a plane and leave the United States.

Despite orders to law enforcement not to shoot, when Jackson, the fugitives and the hostages began pulling away from the area in the van, a vicious gun battle broke out police. Before the shootout was over, the judge, Jonathan Jackson and two of the Soledad Brothers were dead. Two other hostages were wounded, and one of the Soledad Brothers survived.

When investigators discovered that suspended University of California professor and revolutionary Angela Davis had purchased the weapons that Jackson distributed in the courtroom and used in the escape effort, a warrant was issued for her arrest on charges of murder and kidnapping.

Davis was arrested in New York City by the FBI on a federal fugitive warrant on October 13, 1970. She was extradited to California and indicted on counts of murder, kidnapping and conspiracy less than a month later. Davis, who grew up in a middle-class section of Birmingham, Alabama during the 1950s and 1960s, was recognized at a young age for her intelligence and academic brilliance. She attended prestigious boarding schools on scholarship and spent some of her university years at universities in France and Germany. Yet, one of the moments of her education that influenced her later views the most was the bombing of the church she attended in Birmingham. This bombing, perpetrated by white racists, killed four young African-American girls.

The prosecution contended that Davis provided the guns knowingly because she loved George Jackson and wanted him out of prison for personal reasons. Davis' defense team countered by acknowledging that Davis did buy the guns, but they were for her own protection, given the number of death threats she received because of her high profile and radical politics. Davis became the focus of an international campaign to acquit her of all charges and free her. This campaign raised the public awareness of her trial, and by default, the fairness of the judicial system in the United States. She was acquitted on all charges in June of 1972. Many observers are convinced that Davis would not have been acquitted without the campaign to free her.

The Case of the Ramstein Two

Kathleen Cleaver, Communications Secretary of the Black Panther Party, International Section, in Algiers was invited to speak at a Thanksgiving Day Rally in Germany in November 1970. William Burrell and Lawrence Jackson, along with other black GI's, were busy traveling throughout West Germany visiting military installations passing out leaflets urging all black GI's to turn out for the rally. As fast as they could put up a poster the MP's, CID or West German police would tear them down. Tension on all the military bases was high, as the authorities did everything they could to discourage and stop the rally. A few days before Mrs. Cleaver's scheduled arrival Burrell and Jackson were stopped at a gate of Ramstein military base by German guards. In the struggle that followed, shots were fired and the two GIs were arrested. When Mrs. Cleaver showed up at the Frankfurt airport, she was arrested by German authorities on the orders of Interior Minister Genscher. She was immediately expelled from the country and ordered to never return.

The trial of the Ramstein Two, as Burrell and Jackson became known,, developed into a central focus among radical black GI's and the West German student movement. The trial began June 16, 1971 and ended July 12, 1971. Both were found guilty. Burrell was eventually exiled to Algeria. Jackson was sentenced to six years in prison.

Attica Revolt

On September 13, 1971 a massacre by New York State police and other law-enforcement agencies took the lives of thirty-nine men at Attica State Penitentiary. The outcome of a five-day drama, the assault shocked people around the world. The drama began in May 1971 when prisoners at Attica organized the Attica Liberation Faction By July 2, a list of twenty-eight demands had been formulated and submitted to state officials, including Governor Nelson Rockefeller. The demands addressed issues dealing with the prisoners' daily lives. Liberals in the prison administration tried to implement what demands they could on their own, but their attempts were rejected or ignored by the warden and guards.

An uprising began on September 9, after the beating of two prisoners the day before. Within minutes of the initial confrontation, forty guards were held hostage by the inmates, who also took control of a part of the prison known as D Block.

Although the original outbreak had much in common with other prison riots—with inmates beating guards and looting facilities—within an hour the leadership quickly organized some men to guard the hostages from further harm and began listing prisoner demands. Five new demands were added to the original list the Attica Liberation Faction had presented to the governor in July The five new demands included a call for amnesty; the reconstruction of the prison by inmates; immediate negotiation through a team chosen by the inmates and including movement lawyers, sympathetic members of the New York assembly, and journalists, representatives of the Panthers and Young Lords, and Louis Farrakhan of the Nation of Islam; federal intervention to implement the original demands; and transport for those men who wished to resettle in a non-imperialistic country.

An outside negotiating team was organized and, over the next three and a half days, worked with the prisoners and uncooperative state officials to ease the situation. Meanwhile, Governor Rockefeller ordered state police to prepare for a military assault on the prison. On September 13, after negotiations were abruptly ended and a call to surrender from the Commissioner of Corrections office was rejected by the men in D-Yard, the attack began The toll was 39 dead: 30 inmates and 9 of the guards who had been held hostage. Less than half an hour later the uprising was over.

Sources:
Davis, Angela Yvonne (March 1989). *Angela Davis: An Autobiography*. New York City: International Publishers

Voice of the Lumpen. [Frankfurt, Germany]: Revolutionary People's Communications Network, 1(8), October 1971.

Wicker, Tom. *A Time to Die.The Attica Prison Revolt* Haymarket Publishers (repub.) Chicago. 2011

Summer, 1971

Sergeant Major Haywood stood in the barracks doorway of Pioneer Kaserne in Hanau, Germany. It was 4:30 on a Sunday morning in late summer 1971. A fellow NCO stood on each side of him. Their fatigues looked like they had been pressed. The creases were impeccable.

"Get the fuck up now, soldiers!" A few of the men in the barracks stirred in their beds. Most didn't even hear him. "I said get the fuck up! Now!" Haywood and his two assistants began walking down the rows of bunks kicking the foot boards of each. Some who had stirred earlier sat up and began to pull on some clothes. Most men continued to ignore the sergeant and his lackeys. He shouted one more time.

"Get the fuck up and get out of bed! In ten minutes we will be running to the mess hall! Then we will run to church!" The men began to get up. They were muttering but they were waking. "Let's see you at the ends of your beds now!"

Within a minute every single bunk but one had two men standing at attention in front of the foot board. Some had managed to pull on their fatigues, but most were in their skivvies. Haywood walked to the bed furthest from the door. No one stood at attention there.

"McRice! Willard!" Haywood kicked the foot board repeatedly. "Get the hell out of bed! Now!"

Specialist 4 Victor Willard rubbed his eyes and sat up in the top bunk. He had been out smoking hashish until barely an hour earlier. He tumbled out of bed. His bunk-mate did not move. Sergeant Haywood leaned over. He and McRice had quite a history already. Sgt. Haywood just plain did not like this Kansas City nigger. And McRice considered Haywood a racist cracker.

"Mr. McRice!" shouted the Sergeant. He was less than a foot from McRice's face on the pillow, eyes closed. "In nine minutes we will be in formation in front of the barracks. You will join us! Do I make myself clear?" McRice said nothing.

Haywood walked away, muttering to his assistants. At the door, he turned to the men in the barracks and put up five fingers. "Eight minutes to go, you bunch of pussies. In front of the barracks. Bring that faggot McRice with you." The three NCOs left the building. McRice got up and put on his fatigues.

The men stood in formation in front of the barracks. Haywood had them all at attention. He and his assistants walked up and down the lines, inspecting their uniforms. McRice and Willard were the last two to face Haywood. He looked at both of them and spat on the ground.

"Don't you two assholes know what attention means?" He yelled. Neither man moved. Haywood pushed McRice in the chest. He did the same to Willard. Neither man responded. "Both of you assholes will be given Article 15s and will be confined to base for the next month. Do I make myself clear?"

Willard thought about smoking hash. McRice thought about the clubs he liked. He turned his face to the left, spit on the ground, and began to walk away. Willard followed. Haywood yelled at them to come back. They kept walking. The sergeant ran towards them and placed himself directly in front of the two.

"You don't walk away!" He yelled. He pushed McRice harder than before.

"Fuck you." This, from Willard. Haywood looked at him.

"What did you say?"

"Fuck you, Sarge." Haywood hit Willard as hard as he could. McRice noticed a piece of rebar lying on the ground that must have been from where the foundation for a new barracks was being built. He grabbed it and swung at Haywood who was hitting Willard again and again. The rebar smacked the sergeant on the shoulder. Willard took off running. Unfortunately for McRice, two MPs drove by as he was swinging the rebar, jumped from their jeep and tackled him.

Willard was caught at the gate. McRice was charged with assault and sent to the stockade in Mannheim. The authorities tried to get Willard on an assault charge too, but McRice convinced them he was the sole culprit. Victor Willard spent a night in jail on base. When he was released the next day he packed his guitar and civilian clothes and left. Just walked away. AWOL. Absent without fuckin' leave.

Porgy

Porgy was in a lecture hall at Goethe Universität in Frankfurt for a political meeting organized by a German-Black American Solidarity Committee. Other blacks there were a military deserter and a guy named Nkrumah from Ghana. They were representing the Panther paper called *The Voice of the Lumpen*. The meeting was about the recent arrest of Angela Davis in the States and a call for an international campaign to free her. She had been on the run and then got caught. Now the trial was getting started. She was charged with murder in the attempt to get the Soledad Brothers out of a courtroom in California, an attempt which never had a chance. Within minutes the cops were all over the van carrying the hostages and the brothers who were attempting the breakout. That was the quick and brutal end. Angela was on trial because some of the guns used were registered in her name. The real reason was because she was an intelligent and outspoken black woman the cops hated.

There were about thirty people at the meeting. Porgy had expected more, but figured the attendance was sparse because of the late notice. The attendees included some students, including a few nice-looking women, and a couple guys that looked Turkish, probably Gastarbeiter. The rest were older Germans, probably communists. Since Angela was a member of the party in the states, these guys would be funding the campaign. While they waited for the meeting to start, people talked about the recent massacre at Attica State Prison, the murder of George Jackson and the exile of the Ramstein Two brother, Burrell, to Algiers. Even those who thought they had seen everything were taken aback by the Attica killings a week or two earlier. It made the defense of Angela and others even more important.

The meeting began. As the meeting was called to order, a couple guys who looked like GIs walked in. The chair of the meeting was a middle-aged German cat. Porgy was pretty sure he was a professor.

"Guten Abend. Soll ich Englisch oder Deutsch sprechen ?" The German man held up his hand.

"Deutsch?" About ten hands went up. "Englisch?" Twenty hands went up.

The vote was to carry on the meeting in English. Porgy was relieved. His German was okay, but he usually got lost when the debates started.

While basic business regarding procedure was discussed Porgy mused about his circumstances. He thought about the woman named Ana he usually sat with at these meetings. She wasn't present. He had wanted to sleep with her for a while. They had finally gone home together after the last one. He was surprised at his life in Germany. Not only were the German women friendlier than any white girls he knew in the states, the entire feel of things was different. The military was almost soft in Germany. It was certainly a far cry from the military he had grown up with his entire life. The regimentation he was familiar with was certainly lacking along with any pride among the enlistees. Nobody listened to the old guys with stripes at all. That was fine with him.

It was different in Vietnam . Every one hated the fuckin' war, the lifers and the pigs, even though they kept killing for 'em. I know. I was one of 'em. Can't say what changed my mind really, just a general disgust with the whole trip and discoverin' weed and acid didn't change things enough to forget. Seekin' justice always been part of my life, what with my parents being the proud people they were. Dad joined the fuckin' army 'cause he figured it'd be less segregated than civilian life. He hated racists but didn't want to go to jail fighting 'em. Figured the military would treat him more on the basis of his character than the color of his skin. Mom agreed and they took the ride. I guess it was less segregated but I ain't convinced it's any less racist., Dad swallowed the whole damn story hook, line and sinker. America is the greatest and all that crap. I didn't know how to tell him or Mama I feel different. I loved him when he was alive and respect the shit he had to deal with. When you black, crackers are motherfuckers no matter where you run into 'em. The Army got more than its share. Somehow I managed to not piss off any I know. I guess I do my job and that keeps the real assholes quiet. Who knows maybe there is some respect for my dad since a few of the lifers seem to have known him somewhere along the line? Most I met talked highly of him. Even some of the less racist crackers.

Last time I seen him was March last year. After my two tours in Nam they sent me back to California on leave. My next stop was gonna' be Germany but while I was back there in Oakland, hangin' out and meetin' up with some of my buddies and some of the Panthers, Dad died. Him and Ma were living up near Davis near Travis Air Base. After he retired they bought a place next door to the base. I got two more weeks of leave 'cause of his passin'. It was tough burying the old man 'cause I never had nothin' but respect and love for him even if I thought he misunderstood the black man's position in the hierarchy. He knew what he knew and based his life on that. We had a nice burial for him. A wooden casket and we planted him in a church cemetery with a headstone him and Mama had picked out once they found out he had the cancer. One thing Mama told me when we were reminiscing about the places we lived after Dad died was how he insisted I go with him to the bazaar in Peshawar when we was there so that I knew all people wasn't white. We were the only black family on the base. Hell, a lot of the time we was the only black family in the towns Dad got stationed at. When we was in Pakistan, most of the kids seemed pretty much colorblind but some of their parents wouldn't let me in their house. One mother even told Mama the reason I couldn't play with her kids inside the house was because she didn't want nothing stolen. I had a fifth grade thing with this blonde girl who got beat pretty bad when her Daddy discovered us kissing. We wasn't nothing but ten years old but it was 1960 or 61. Not that nowadays is much different for most folks. My dad was pissed at me not because she was white he said but because I shouldn't be kissing no girls at ten years old. After that I didn't kiss a girl until I was in high school.

After buryin' Dad, I went back to Oakland. While I was there I had some fun times with old friends of mine that never went into the service. Their numbers were too high or they had too many busts on their sheet. They lived in Oakland 'cause that's where the hustlers and the women at. There was a lot more happening there than in Davis . Tryin' to talk politics with 'em wasn't easy but I think they heard me a bit. Mostly they didn't pay no attention. Some of the political comrades tell me I should be contemptuous of my bros' playin' the game set up by the man to keep 'em in chains, but what good would it do? They still my brothers.

Victor

Victor walked through the Speyer rock festival crowd. He had been smoking hash most of the night and was very stoned. Deep Purple was playing onstage. Four weeks had passed since he left his unit, and Victor was still paranoid about being recognized by a former barracks mate, much less undercover military police. What better place to get lost then a rock festival crowd, especially one including thousands of GIs. He didn't look out of place. Another hit of acid would help him stay awake. The field where the stage was must be a hundred acres, with beer and soda bottles in piles everywhere. It had yet to rain like it usually seemed to do at these affairs. Hundreds of tents were set up in the concert field. Although some cars were in the concert area, most of them were parked on the road. People just took their gear and walked in. Looking around last night as he walked aimlessly, high on hashish, acid and some bubbly wine, he was reminded of his uncle's farm in Indiana. There were trees here and there, a small stream, and lots of open space. The farm was where he spent most of his high school years after his dad died in the truck accident. Mom began hanging out in bars and bringing home whomever she ended up with to the little house they lived in with the dog Betsy and the cat that everybody just called Cat. His uncle, his dad's older brother, was at one of the bars Mom went to and she tried to pick him up. She was so drunk or high or whatever she didn't even recognize him. Or so she said. That was enough for Uncle Jack. He started working on getting custody the next day. She always did talk about how her brother-in-law thought he was holier than Jesus.

Victor spent the next five years on the farm. He went to school in town and bought pot there but mostly he worked on the farm until the Army drafted him. He and Uncle Jack watched the fucking lottery on television. It was July 1st, 1970. Victor's birthdate was July 25th and his number came up third. There was no way in hell he was not going to be drafted. If he had known more about the law he might have been able to get out of the draft since he was the only surviving son but there weren't any draft counselors in rural Indiana. So off he went. There were a few times he went to Chicago to see concerts. Cream was the only band he actually remembered. After hearing them jam on the song "Crossroads" he bought a Silvertone guitar and amp from the Sears catalog and taught himself to play.

At the rock festival I met this chick named Ana. A

stone fox, with black hair and blue eyes. She took me home and I've been staying with her in a squatted building in Frankfurt called Roter Stern Kommune. It's kind of ironic with it being across the street from the fuckin' PX. The building's got a nice set up with stolen electricity and running water. Apparently the city can't legally turn the water off in a building where people live even if they are there illegally. There's lots of apartments turned into bigger rooms by knocking out some walls. The kitchens are huge. It's mostly political freaks living there. There's lots of hashish and posters everywhere including one of that Uschi Obermaier chick where she's nude. I've been doing a lot of cooking and cleaning since Ana doesn't want me going out because I'm AWOL. Still, I ended up at a meeting last week about Angela Davis. There were a couple brothers there. GIs. It all seemed right on.

Ana is the first girl I've ever really been with. Like I said, she's a fox. I can't believe my luck every time I lay down next to her. I had a girlfriend in high school but we never did anything but kiss and smoke pot. She was afraid of getting pregnant and I was afraid of getting her pregnant. There wasn't any birth control I knew of around. The girls since then have just been friends. You know, people to get high with and so on. I'm still not sure how Ana and me ended up together. It was Saturday night at the rock fest. It was in between Deep Purple and whoever came after them, if anybody even did come after them. I just couldn't walk no more I was so fucking tired. So I just sat down in some circle of people around a fire. They were drinking whiskey and smoking hash. I think I drank some whiskey and crashed out. It was getting light when I woke up. My breath tasted terrible and I had a blanket over me. After some of the pain in my head subsided, I sat up. Ana was opposite me and was stirring the embers of the fire trying to get it going again. People were crashed out all around and one guy was sitting by himself looking all wild. His eyes were like that Russian guy Rasputin's and his hair had sticks and grass in it. Probably took too much acid. I looked at Ana and smiled. She smiled back. Then I went and found some wood to burn. The festival promoters had put small piles of firewood at various places in the field. Where we were was close to one of them. Ana and I got the fire going and I went to sit next to her. I wished I still had my guitar but I'd sold it for food and beer. She didn't mind. We made some tea and drank it. She speaks English pretty good. I found some hash in my pocket and she had a bottle of wine. We started in on getting high and ended up hanging out the rest of the weekend. Then she got me a ride with her friends back to Frankfurt. Like I said I go to meetings with her sometimes although the politics kind of bores me. I'm into fucking with the system and all but talking about it seems like school.

I hate to think about what Uncle Jack would say if he knew the shit I was in. Fuck. AWOL. Plus, I'm probably wanted as an accomplice with McRice smacking that asshole sergeant upside his head. Speaking of McRice he took me to a whorehouse in Frankfurt once. I didn't do nothing except walk around and look at all the mostly naked women. The place was legal and reminded me of a parking garage with a bunch of rooms and everything bathed in purple light. The women called out hey come fuck. Some of them were pretty but like I said I didn't do anything but look. It just didn't seem right to me, those women selling themselves like they were sides of beef instead of real live, pretty girls. McRice and his friends went into a room with a few of the hookers and came out an hour or so later while I drank beer and talked pigeon German with a blonde girl. Here I am hanging out with a bunch of people who call themselves communist. I bet Uncle Jack would wish he tried to keep me out of the service like I asked him to. No, though. He said I needed some discipline — like getting up every damn day at 4 in the morning to help him out in the barn wasn't discipline. He ain't a bad guy but just so stuck in his ways. I guess farming does that to people. You kind of lose touch with change since everything, even change, has a routine to it on the farm. You know when the crops are coming in, when the calves are going be born and when you gotta plant the seed. Change all the time but natural like instead of all the sudden you're on the fuckin' lam from the military and living with some foxy German chick in a commune full of

German freaks. I sure as hell didn't expect that. Hell, I didn't even plan on going to the rock festival where I met her.

Later that week, Victor was in a place in downtown Frankfurt called the Zoom Club. It was a primary venue for touring rock, blues and jazz bands not quite popular enough to fill a hall. It had been the site of some incredible music. In addition, local musicians, both German and American played there. Hashish was smoked openly and trading in it was almost as obvious. Consequently, it was off-limits to GIs. Victor was spending more time there than ever, making some money selling hash and acid. Ana liked both and consumed either when she wasn't doing political stuff. It was smart not to be high when she was in the streets. There seemed to be a lot of dope in every room at the commune where they lived, though. The cops had to know. Lately there seemed to be more heroin and speed at Zoom. Ana and other leftists saw the influx of hard stuff as a conspiracy to destroy the movement. Victor tried to stay away from both. He mostly smoked hashish. Speed didn't really set with him, and heroin just had a fear that came with its temptation. So far, whatever allure it had was not too tempting. Meanwhile, the sound guys had asked him to help out. It wasn't for much pay but he did get free drinks and music. Ana could also come in for free whenever she wanted to.

Ana

After that meeting Victor attended, a few of us had gone to a Gasthaus in the Westend. It was in a besetzendtes Haus. What do you call it? A squat? I think it was Victor, myself, Porgy, a student named Martin and one of the Black Panthers. I know the people that operate the Gasthaus so they didn't make us pay for the beer. After everyone had a beer to drink, Porgy asked the Black Panther guy about an article on the Ramstein Two in the Voice of the Lumpen. I learned most of my English from reading that paper and others like it. Victor did not say anything during the whole conversation. Then he took out a pipe and we smoked some hashish. The Black Panther started to talk about the Ramstein Two. This was the case that made me want to be involved with the Amerikanisch black liberation movement. Before that I was primarily engaged in antiwar protests and the Hausbesetzung movement.

"So Kathleen Cleaver was scheduled to speak at Goethe Universität on Thanksgiving." The Black Panther began. "She was coming in on a plane and me and this brother from Ghana were supposed to pick her up. You remember Eldridge was in Algeria then. That fuckin' hippie Timothy Leary had just moved into the compound down there. I always questioned that move. Why bring the heat that son of a bitch had following him? Anyhow, these two brothers named Burrell and Jackson was pasting up leaflets and meeting with brothers all over Germany trying to get a good showing for Kathleen. The pigs already had their eye on them two 'cause they weren't shy about their shit. Some of us who had already been through the military pig scene was counseling them to be a little more low key but you know how the youngsters can be. Not that they are that much younger in years but I'm talkin' about experience, you see what I'm sayin'? So they was trying to get into one of the gates at Ramstein air base and all hell broke loose when some pigs tried to stop 'em. I was against the idea of our people packing, but got overruled. If they hadn't had those guns they wouldn't have shot at the pigs but then they might have just got offed, so you see it's hard to tell who was correct on the gun question.

"Next thing we know up in the main office was that them two was in a German jail and waiting to be turned over to the military. We got them some lawyers quick but they went to the brig. Kathleen landed at Rhein Main civilian and barely got off the plane before that fucker Genscher sent her out of the country."

Genscher is the Interior Minister. He is a real

schwein who hates leftists. Just another Nazi in the government. I am serious, he was in the Wehrmacht. He is the one who designed the repressive political laws that start in 1972. I remember how we organized for Kathleen. Every day we were at the places where the GIs drink beer. We talked mostly with the black men but also with the hippie white GIs. The MPs would chase us away when they saw us in the Gasthäuser. I think they were very afraid of a rebellion. I gave out hundreds of leaflets every week for a month before the arrests. After the news of the refusal to let Kathleen into Deutschland reached the GIs, I thought there will be a riot very soon. I think the military police thought so too. They made the GIs stay on base and they have shut down some of the Gasthäuser where we would meet them. In Höchst an office was set on fire. No one was ever verhaftet. Arrested?

The room was full of people. It was not very loud. The smoke from cigaretten and hashish was not too bad. The stereo played Amon Duul. It is a small space, twenty metern by thirty, vielleicht. Porgy was sitting on one side of me and Victor on the other. I did not think too much about it until later when Porgy asked me to go with him to the cinema sometime soon. I hesitated when I answered and told him I would think about it. Victor was talking with a hippie GI. One wall has a painting on it. It shows the women of Vietnam and some scenes from the struggle for civil rights in Amerika and is very beautiful. Some-

times a show is at the place. Victor said he went to a FTA show once there. I meet GIs who want to leave the army here sometimes. It is a safe space for them, at least until now. I like Victor more than I usually like Americans. I like Porgy, who is very smart and good in bed, but the way I feel about Victor is different. Usually Americans do not interest me except for a night or two. Honest. I brought Victor home because I wanted him to desert to Sweden, but he is not interested. Then I started to like him. He is very much like I think Americans are. What is the word? Naiv auf Deutsch. He makes me think of Huckleberry Finn's friend. Tom Sawyer? Not like Huckleberry who is worldly compared with Tom. He says that he loves me and does not want to go to Sweden where he would be lonely. I think I love him also. When he made the fire at the rock festival and we drank tea I think I fell in love. That is verrückt. Crazy. I don't know him at all. Until then.

He wants to know why I am so political. I try and tell him it is because my father was a Nazi and we cannot let that happen again. I don't know if he understands. Americans I have met do not understand politics very well. They are moral people but do not understand power. My father was not a big man in the Nazi party. He joined so he could keep his job and then he went into the Wehrmacht. He fought in the East. I have been born two years after the war has ended. My father met my mother at a camp that the

Amis had set up for refugees. He did not tell her that he had been in Wehrmacht. The Amis found out and brought him to a different camp but my mother was pregnant when they took him. I think they must have had a friend in the occupier forces because they were able to send letters to each other and after my father was let go they married and moved to Rödelheim. This is a small town next to Frankfurt. The Number 3 Strassenbahn goes there. I grew up on Kirschbaum-weg for 16 years. My father worked at a paint factory for many years. The town always smelled like the paint. I went to university when I was 17 and moved to Bockenheim. My father died two years ago and my mother moved to an apartment in Offenbach. She is not happy with me. I think she is mostly afraid. She remembers the Nazis and the war. She does not trust the police to be different now. Neither do I but I think we must fight to keep the Nazis from returning.

Victor

It had been two years at least since I drove a car. Ana borrowed a friend's Opel Kadett so that we could take a day and drive around. Driving was a piece of cake. We pulled together thirty marks, a chunk of hash and a big bottle of strawberry wine. The first place we went was to Sachsenhausen to drink some Apfelwein. The stuff is a little sour but it gave me a nice buzz. Then we headed up to the Taunus Mountains where we found a castle and walked around. Smoked some hash in the moat and kissed. After that we found some woods and made love for a while. Smoked some more hash and made some more love. By then we were pretty fucking hungry so we found a Gasthaus and ate and drank. I love those smoked pork chops and that rotkraut that seems to be a standard meal around here. We found a place on a mountain with a clear view west and watched the sun set while we drank and smoked. I wish that's all we ever did. Smoke, drink and fuck.

You know, my uncle wasn't a harsh man. In fact he was probably the nicest older man I ever met. Of course, when you consider the competition it's easy to see why. Most of my school teachers were ex-drill sergeants that didn't know the Army had let them go. Then the next bunch of older men I ran into were the assholes in the military. Talk about fucked in the head. I am so glad I walked away from it no matter what happens. Anyhow, Uncle Jack was pretty laid back. Sure he made me do chores on the farm but I never really minded except for maybe the first few months and that was probably because I was so pissed at my mom for being such a loser and at my dad for dying. It wasn't his fault. I never remember him yelling at me or hitting me. He was pretty firm in his beliefs and ways but I never really tried to challenge him by doing stuff in his house that he disapproved of. It's like I wanted him to like and respect me because I respected him. So much so that I even went to church with him most of the time.

Last time I saw him was probably the only time I had real fun with him since before my dad died. Not that he wasn't fun, but he was always a business first kind of guy. I was back from boot camp for a couple weeks. Then I was shipping out to Germany. I was just happy it wasn't Vietnam. That was only the second time I had been drinking with my uncle. The other time was the day I turned 18. My uncle parked the car near the One Spot Tavern just as I put out the Camel I'd been smoking on the ride from the farm. We got out, went in and started drinking and playing pool with these two old guys. Ended up spending the entire night there drinking and talkin' with 'em. I left for Germany a couple days later.

Ana

Ana came up the escalator from the U-Bahn tracks. She was in the Hauptwache, on the same level as the record store where she worked. There were several other stores accessible from this level. One was the Kaufhof that the ultraleftists around Andreas Baader firebombed a few years ago. There was also a Konditorei and a few other clothing stores. It was late evening. She reached the top of the escalator and looked around. The guy she was looking for was supposed to be in the little alcove across from the escalator where the hippies smoked hash during the day while the police were busy with other things. She saw him. His hair was parted in the middle like so many hippie GIs. He wore bell-bottom jeans and a turtleneck under his leather jacket. She turned left and made a slight motion with her head. He followed and called out her code name Uschi. Smiling, she turned to him as if they were old friends. After hugging quickly, they walked away side by side.

His name was Daniel Miller. The plan was to get him on a train into Sweden. He was still in the service but had obtained a couple weeks of leave and was ready to get out. Before being stationed in Frankfurt Daniel had been in Vietnam. He still had eighteen months left in his enlistment but was not willing to complete it. Ana was part of a group that helped GIs desert. It was connected to some antiwar organizations in the United States, Germany and Sweden. Daniel would be the tenth person she helped out and this would be his last meeting before leaving. They came up into the night air from the underground and headed to a small bar near the Hauptbahnhof. It was called Hot Times and catered to GIs and Gastarbeiter even though the military authorities had placed it off limits. The regulars included hookers, pimps, small time hashish dealers, and a few Yugoslavs and Turks that liked to drink strong coffee and ouzo. It was in a part of the city easily classified as between sleazy and seedy. Hot Times leaned toward seedy. Hookers did not openly ply their trade in the bar. It seemed to Ana that both prostitutes and dealers used the place as a haven from the police and the market found on the street and in other bars and clubs nearby. The truth of the matter was that it was a front for an organized crime group that operated throughout Europe, smuggling people and hashish. Behind the bar was a guy who was more of an anarchist than anything and seemed to enjoy the people that came through his door. Hot Times was one of three places that the deserter group used to meet up with prospective deserters.

Ana and Daniel were on Grosse Gallusstrasse. The Hauptbahnhof was a few blocks away. Hot Times was in an alley located off of Kaiserstrasse. The bartender was pretty good at smelling out undercover cops and had his own ways of dealing with them. If Daniel was a policeman he would probably wish that he had never taken the assignment after the bartender and his men were through with him. They walked into the bar and headed to a table in the back. When the waitress came to the table. Daniel ordered two beers.

"Uschi." He began. "I am looking forward to my vacation." He took out his passport.

"Put that away," whispered Ana. "Wait until we have finished this beer." She needed a minute or two to scope out the place. If there were any problems, the bartender would let her know through a wink or some other signal. They drank their beers. "Do you like Emerson, Lake and Palmer?"

"Yeah," answered Daniel. "I saw them the last time they played here. I'm a big fan of Keith Emerson. I loved his stuff with The Nice."

"Me, too," agreed Ana. The beer tasted good. Daniel finished his and made a motion for another. He knew that he would be on a train for quite a while and figured on sleeping through the first part of the trip at least. "You have bought your tickets all the way to Stockholm?"

Daniel nodded yes.

"Your passport is good with the visas?"

He nodded again.

"When you reach the Bahnhof in Stockholm there will be a black man waiting for you at the milk bar. His name is Thomas and he has been in Stockholm for two years. He will help you find friends and a job when the time is right. He will introduce you to people who will help you apply for asylum," Ana continued. "You cannot come back to any country that Amerika has troops in, you understand? Maybe if you change your name someday that will be possible."

Daniel nodded his head again. There was no reason to come back to Germany. As for the United States, his mother was dead and his father was a drunken bigot Daniel had little to do with. He joined the service just to get away from him. When Daniel brought the paper from the recruiter for his dad to sign, they were both glad to know that they would no longer have to look at each other. He and Ana drank another beer. Daniel gave her five marks for the beer and got up. Ana hugged him and wished him luck.

"Thanks, Uschi." He picked up his backpack and left. The first train he had to catch left at 22 Uhr. Uschi waited twenty minutes and headed back to the U-Bahn.

One more Ami out of the military. I always feel better when I have helped a GI leave. Politically it is a victory and we have removed one more person from their imperialist machine. On a personal level, I think

She walked out on Taunusstrasse where the evening was well underway. Prostitutes and barkers for sex clubs were trying to get people to buy what they were selling. The neon flashed everywhere. Turks, Greeks and Yugoslavs--who made up the bulk of the Gastarbeiter in Frankfurt--walked along the street in small groups. Many of them lived in small pensions that catered to the Gastarbeiter population. Many of these pensions charged exorbitant rates that the workers could do very little about because of their legal status and the language barrier. There were several coffee shops and bars where music from the Gastarbeiter home countries played on the jukeboxes. GIs walked around in their jeans looking for dope and sex. The majority of the GIs that wandered around this part of town were black since so many of the clubs in other parts of town discriminated against their color.

I met my first American here when I was 18. I was passing out leaflets for a protest against repression of

The Hauptwache was just ahead. Ana walked across the plaza to the Strassenbahn stops. She was taking number 3 back to Bockenheimer Warter for another meeting at the university. This one was about a rumored police raid on the squats in the Westend. Real estate speculators were stepping up the pressure on the city to clear out the squatters so they could complete the sale of the apartment buildings. Once sold, they would be converted into much more profitable office space. The authorities' preparations for the rumored raids were military-like. Police were stockpiling tear gas and a variety of other weapons and ammunition. In response, the squatters were building defenses of their own. These included bricks, stones, trip wires and slingshots. Some squatters were building structures so they could launch garbage and boiling water from the roofs of the buildings. For Ana, the best thing about these meetings was that there was no need to convince people of the need for action and nobody's politics was in question. These were all about tactics.

Victor

Victor wasn't sure how it got to this. First, a little bit of the powder in a hash pipe with the hash. Then a snort; smoking opium with some little ratty guy at Red Star while everyone else was at a meeting discussing rumors about a police raid on the squats. Even a shot once, though he had always said he hated needles. Just like a drug education movie put out by the army. He could blame it on Ana and her being too busy with the planning for Angela's sister's rally but he knew that was bullshit. So he blamed it on the military. Although they certainly deserved some blame, it was mostly his fault. He just didn't care about anything enough, not even Ana. He still believed she didn't know he used.

He had never been to war so that was no excuse. There was no real reason to use other than boredom.

I have dreams like I was there though. In one I'm with a platoon or a squad and we're going into villages and burning down huts. The last village we enter the killing and burning is especially gruesome. The screams we hear are more than typical death screams.

It was Christmas time. Victor was discovering the
holiday period was a big deal in Germany. He was
with Ana in downtown Frankfurt at a place called An
der Roemer, the location of the city hall building and
a plaza. They walked through the Christmas market.
The old buildings were dwarfed by skyscrapers built
in the past few years. Numerous aromas permeated
the air: the smell of the Glühwein and the chestnuts,
wurst and the sweets, wood smoke and the pine
wreaths. Ana told him how much her mother loved
the market. It was very important to their holidays
together. When she was a girl her aunt's friend who
she called Onkel sold chestnuts there. Frankfurt was
still a bombed-out city then, especially down near the
Main River. Onkel had a roasting contraption made
from a steel barrel, tongs and little paper cones. He
still gave her free chestnuts. Victor had never tasted
roasted chestnuts until now. He wondered what On-

kel thought of him. He had to be used to Ana having boyfriends that looked like hippies.

She never talked much about her life before she left home and Victor had never asked. It seemed to him from those rare occasions she even mentioned it that she and her dad had been fairly close and when he passed, she dove into politics even deeper than before. He put his hand around her waist and pulled her close. Ana kissed him and smiled.

Porgy

The Ghetto Poets were rehearsing. "Niggers are scared of revolution…." The drum beat intensified. Porgy smiled and tapped the conga in front of him. They were doing a Last Poets song at the Free Angela rally in a few weeks and they needed some rehearsing. The girls from the high school had their lyrics and moves down but all the brothers were just jiving.

I just wanna' look good in front of the crowd.,. Shit, it's gonna' be the biggest crowd we performed in front of yet. Even bigger than the GURUGURU con- cert at the university. Talk about fun, my man. After we was done with our version of "Stand," the crowd went wild. There must have been five hundred people there. We play that Sly song unique. Just percussion. No guitar or piano. Talking drums, congas and some snare is all. It sounds real bad and always gets people dancing. Masses dig it.

Porgy never saw himself as a musician. In fact he joined the group to spread a political message. He had to admit that watching audiences react to the music made him appreciate the music side of the act more.

After joining, he stayed for the message and because he was interested in a young woman in the group named Martha. An officer's daughter, her hair was natural and she usually wore it in an afro like Angela. Sometimes though, she braided it, which truly turned Porgy on. They had gone out a couple times yet there was a part of him that remained hesitant to make any moves because of her dad's rank. Martha had just turned eighteen and had a scholarship to Yale. The time for him to do anything was growing short. He would be getting out of the military this coming fall. They were going out leafleting together tomorrow. The Free Angela committee had put together a leaflet that was written in English on one side and German on the other. Their first stop to distribute them would be the shop near Edwards Kaserne where a lot of black GIs congregated on the weekends. The shop had pool tables, a jukebox with a lot of soul music, beer and German women. The leaflets described Angela's case (as if everybody didn't already know about it) and invited folks to join in the campaign to free her. It also mentioned the possibility of Angela's sister Fania making a stop in Frankfurt in the next couple months. From what Porgy knew, the tour was definitely going to happen. The planners in various cities were currently figuring out Fania's itinerary. Others were dealing with making sure she could get into the country. Unlike Kathleen Cleaver, who never actually left the airport when she tried to visit the previous year, Fania had no criminal record.

Porgy wasn't sure that Kathleen did, but the Germans used that as an excuse to keep her out of the country.

The next morning Porgy waited for Martha in the U-Bahn stop by the PX. He had a box of 2000 leaflets. The text was concise and clear, with the picture of Angela turning out nicely. He smoked a cigarette while he waited. The posters on the wall opposite him announced an old concert by King Crimson at the Zoom Club. Porgy knew of the band from their album covers. Once when he was on some acid, he had stared at the one called *Court of the Crimson King* for hours. The artwork showed the cavernous mouth of something that was probably the Crimson King. The colors of the painting were purple, pink and a few other shades. Next to the concert poster was a call for a protest against the Turkish government. All Porgy knew about Turkey's politics was that the fascists were in control there and were imprisoning the leftists en masse.

"Hey, Porgy." Martha smiled as she walked up the stairs from the tracks. She gave him a hug and stepped back.

"Hey, sister." Porgy smiled. "How you doin'?"

"Good. What we got?" Martha nodded at the box of leaflets. Porgy pulled one out and handed it to her. "Looks good, huh?"

"Yeah." She grabbed a handful with one hand, tucked them under her arm and took Porgy's hand with her other hand. "Let's hit the PX parking lot first."

"You sure?" Hesitated Porgy. "We're supposed to head to Edwards."

"It's cool. We'll just give them out to the brotherss in the cafeteria. We can spare half an hour. We got time." Porgy shrugged his shoulders and went with Martha to the cafeteria. The place was packed. Most everybody there was either a GI or teenage dependent. It was the perfect crowd to pass the leaflets out to. It took fifteen minutes to put one in every person's hand. When they were done they went back to the U-Bahn. A couple of stops later they disembarked and caught a Strassenbahn to Edwards Kaserne. The Kaserne was perhaps ten city blocks surrounded by a cement wall. The surrounding neighborhood included taverns that catered to GIs, some small shops and a German supermarket. Everything was smiles and laughter between them. Their trip on the streetcar was brief. When they got off they were immediately approached by two military policemen.

"You can't take those on to the Kaserne," said one of the MPs, pointing at the leaflets.

"We weren't planning to," responded Porgy.

"Let me see one." Martha gave one to the MP requesting a leaflet. He looked at it briefly, folded it in half and put it in his pants pocket. Porgy started to say something, but stopped.

"Don't let me see you near the gate or inside the Kaserne with those things," warned the MP that had spoken before. They got back in their jeep and drove away. By this time a small crowd had gathered. Martha and Porgy passed out leaflets to anyone that would take one. Soon, a discussion was underway among a number of black and white GIs about Angela. Porgy and Martha continued to pass out leaflets while they joined in. Within half an hour, all of the leaflets were gone. There were no further incidents with the MPs or anybody else opposed to their presence.

Victor

It had always felt weird to Victor being in someone else's country, especially given the haircuts and clothes the military had to wear. It must be even harder for the black guys. Victor thought about this while he sat in the park near Eschenheimer Turm. The guard tower that the park was named after was part of the old city's system of defense. Now the park was known as Hash Park because it was one of the easiest places to score dope in Frankfurt. Some of the people hanging out were pretty shady. He had never really known much about heroin and other hard drugs, but most of what he knew he had learned in this park. The first time he had ever been in the park was back in February before a Pink Floyd concert at the Festhalle. He and the guy they called Zonker scored some incredible window-pane acid from a German hippie dealer. The acid hit them on their way back to the concert hall. The streetlights dripped and the crosswalks were difficult to navigate. Victor watched a couple GIs coming towards him.

"Hey, Willard!" One of the GIs flashed a peace

sign at Victor. The two were from Victor's old unit. Shit, this could be trouble, thought Victor.

"How's it goin'?" Victor and the two men shook hands, doing a white guy version of the soul brothers dap. Instead of being long and drawn out, this handshake involved a thumb grip and then a conventional shake. Victor was a little nervous even though he knew these guys were cool. What if the cops had put them up to finding him by threatening them with a bust?

"Good, man." Said the GI named Will. Victor remembered the other guy's name as Jon. "Long time no see."

"Let's walk," said Victor. The three men began walking down a path away from the park and towards a section of town full of alleys and cobblestone streets. "I'm a little paranoid, as you can well imagine." All three of the men laughed.

"Fuck man," said Will. "You and McRice changed some shit around in the fuckin' unit."

"Yeah," Jon added. "Haywood is gone back to the world and the new CO is a pretty decent guy for a lifer. He don't fuck with us like Haywood did. No more early morning inspections and no more of that fuckin' church."

Victor listened as the two men described the new regime at the barracks and in the unit. Apparently, the Army had replaced Haywood's old guard with some NCOs that spoke the new language of the Army. The keywords in that language included tolerance, less punishment and some minimal respect for the enlisted men. This was something Victor had heard about while he was in but never seen. The primary reason behind the whole liberalized approach was to prevent GIs from deserting and to get youngsters to enlist. He figured it would last until the generals figured out how to crack down again. Part of the reason for the changes could be laid on the efforts of antiwar people trying to unionize the military, but for the most part it was about pulling the rug out from those people and their efforts.

"That's cool," joked Victor. "I still don't think they would let me back in."

"Nah," agreed Jon. "You can bet they want your ass even though you didn't do anything. Fuck, I couldn't believe it that morning when Haywood hit you and I really couldn't believe it when McRice nailed him on the shoulder with that rebar. That was crazy. Crazy but kind of cool."

"Whatever happened to McRice?" Asked Victor.

"They said he attacked Haywood for no reason and gave him six months I think," answered Will. "I don't know what kind of discharge he'll end up getting. You know they fucked with him bad. They never liked that brother."

"Let's go in here." Victor opened the door to a small bar he knew was safe from prying eyes. The men sat down and ordered some beer. Victor noticed that both men had sideburns and hair that was longer than regulation. His former unit must really have loosened up. The new CO must be all right for a lifer. Hair was always one of Haywood's pet peeves. Victor had done lots of extra duty over hair length.

"So," asked Will. "What have you been doin' man? How do you survive?"

Victor was paranoid about saying too much but these two seemed like they just wanted to know, so he filled them in a little. "I work a little at the Zoom Club doing techie stuff. I sell a little bit of hash and I smoke a lot. I'm living with this German chick I met at the rock fest on that island."

"Yeah. We were there," nodded Will. "It was pretty good. I was happy to see Fairport Convention. And The Faces. Jon here got so fuckin' wasted we missed our ride back."

"I figure sooner or later I am going to have to figure out something more long term but, hey, the world might end tomorrow so whatever..." Victor shrugged his shoulders and ordered another beer. The three men drank a couple more beers and talked about music and drugs. Then Will and Jon paid the bill. After one more handshake, they parted ways.

"Maybe we'll see you at a show, man," said Will as he and Jon walked away. Victor flashed the peace sign and went in the other direction.

That was kind of cool, he thought, like they were interested and kind of surprised to see me. Still, he was glad they had no idea where he lived. He reminded himself to be more careful at Zoom Club, just in case either Jon or Will were asked by the cops where to find him. Heading back to the park, he thought about the movie he was seeing with Ana this evening. There was a theater that was in a small courtyard between Eschenheimer Turm and the Roemer that they liked to go to. Sometimes, he spent all day there watching films. It was one of those kinds of theaters that held film festivals featuring different directors and actors. The people that hung out in the place were mostly students and longhairs. The first movie they had seen together was that Mick Jagger flick *Performance*. Victor found it to be an incredibly weird yet cool film. He had seen it maybe four more times since then. At first his favorite scene was the one where Mick is in the tub with Anita Pallenberg and a little French chick. After Ana teased him about how that was such a conventional male fantasy he was able to meditate more on the film's meaning. It was mostly about death and the corruption of money. Ana was fascinated with the mushroom trip and the stuff Jagger's character says right before it. Then there was the Stones song Memo from Turner about the corruption of power and capitalism, another really good blues rock tune. The movie playing that evening was an Andy Warhol flick. It was guaranteed to be weird. When they were at the movies it was like they were all alone. The only other time he felt like that was when they were making love.

Victor sat in the back of a coffee shop near the Hauptwache. The place was full of Turks and Yugoslavs playing pinball and drinking coffee. The conversations rose and fell according to whatever the hell they were discussing. The time was right around 3 in the afternoon. He was supposed to meet a guy named Tarachi in a few minutes. Tarachi was the son of the Turkish Consul in Frankfurt who smuggled hashish into Germany using his dad's diplomatic pouch. Then he brought acid back to Turkey and sold it to the Turks. He was quite a character who had an air of invincibility about him that was hard to resist. People Victor knew told stories about crazy shit they did when hanging out with Tarachi because they felt no fear. The life of a diplomat's son had convinced Tarachi that he could not be brought down. Victor hoped that this would hold true as long as he dealt with him. The hashish he brought in was the best he had ever smoked. It was a reddish green color that supposedly came from Lebanon or Syria and had an incredibly sweet taste.

The coffee Victor was drinking had his knees jumping. Turkish coffee was always strong but this particular cup was extraordinarily so. It certainly intensified his nervousness. Having only met Tarachi briefly, he was hoping he would remember what he looked like in a room full of his countrymen. The jukebox had a selection of songs from Turkey, some Arab music and the Rolling Stones. While he waited, Victor recalled the Stones concert he had attended earlier in the year. He and a buddy had bought tickets at the store in the IG Farben Building. Once they heard that the Stones were playing their last tour in Great Britain they knew they had to go. The reason the Stones were leaving Britain had something to do with taxes. Victor lucked into tickets for the opening show in Newcastle. The band played lots of songs from their newest album. Victor's favorite was probably "Wild Horses." If one wanted a definition of what country blues sounded like, they just needed to listen to that song. Since that tour, the Stones had moved to France and made another album.

Victor was glad to recognize Tarachi walking through the door of the shop, just as he finished his second cup of coffee, After stopping at the counter and buying a coffee, Tarachi scanned the shop for Victor. Once he spotted him Tarachi made a signal asking if he wanted something to drink. Victor shook his head no. Tarachi paid for the coffee and walked over to Victor's table. He sat down.

"Hey, man." Tarachi greeted Victor. His English was spectacular, having learned it in high schools in New York State.

"How are you?" Asked Victor.

"I'm good." Tarachi extended his hand. "Let me drink the coffee and we'll go into the back room. I know the family that owns this shop and they let me use their office."

Victor nodded. He had been wondering exactly how they were going to do the deal. After Tarachi finished his cup of coffee, he stood and walked toward the back of the store. Victor followed. Once they were in the room and the door was locked, Tarachi pulled out a nice-looking brick of hashish.

"Two kilos minus a little bit I smoked." Said Tarachi. "Just to make sure I was getting what I wanted."

"Sure." said Victor. "No problem. The money has already been agreed upon, right?"

"Yeah. You got it?." Victor handed him the cash fronted to him by his customers. Even through the foil Victor could smell the potency of the drug.. "Do you want to smoke some?"

Victor nodded. Tarachi pulled a pipe from his pocket, softened a small piece of hashish with a flame, packed it into the pipe, and lit it. When they were finished smoking, they sat down in the office and relaxed. After a few minutes, Tarachi went into the desk in the room and pulled out a bottle of arak. He poured two small glasses and they drank. Leaving the glasses on the desk and stashing the bottle, he motioned to Victor that they should leave. Victor followed Tarachi out of the office and headed toward the door of the shop. Tarachi went to a pinball machine and began playing. Victor left. His next stop was to the Roter Stern to cut the chunk of hash into six pieces, then to the Zoom Club where his buyers waited.

Tarachi waited until Victor was gone before he left. He planned to take a train back to Istanbul and was looking forward to the trip.

Victor was a little nervous. This deal was the biggest one yet. Two kilos of hash. He knew most of the buyers but had to admit that he was unsure about a couple of them. However, he had sold to the others a few times and all of them seemed cool. They were all German hippie types that liked his prices. The fact that Tarachi's product was better than every other product around also helped his cause. If the deal went down smoothly he would make two thousand marks in profit. That would set him up for a couple months and he wouldn't need to deal.

He planned to meet the buyers at Zoom Club in between sets. There was a band composed of high school guys named Shady Grove playing that night. He wasn't sure who they were opening for but that didn't matter because he planned to be back at the commune very soon after the deal went down. While waiting in the back of the club he sipped on a Coke and ate a falafel from the Turkish place down the street. He and Ana had spent the afternoon making love. She was now at her mother's place. No use in freaking her out about shit she didn't need to know. Her political activity was enough to keep her paranoid. In the last three weeks she had helped two guys desert. Furthermore, someone had firebombed some

MP jeeps at the motor pool in Höchst and called in a message saying the deed was done in support of the movement to free Angela and all political prisoners. Of course, this meant the police were watching her political friends more intently than they were watching Victor, the small time hash dealer. The group now known in the mainstream as the Baader-Meinhof Gang had begun robbing banks. Their actions were also drawing the police to the politicos. Baader-Meinhof reminded Victor of the Weather Underground except they seemed to be even crazier, robbing banks and killing cops.

The first band was onstage. Victor knew a couple of the musicians and liked their choice of songs. The fact they had made the cut at Zoom meant their playing was more than competent. The guitarist and drummer would probably go far if they put their minds to it. Victor wished he still had his guitar. The acoustic he played around on at the commune was okay but he missed his electric one. The first song played was the Clapton tune "Tales of the Great Ulysses." It reminded Victor of high school. He and his buddies borrowed a car from somebody's mom and drove to Chicago to see Cream, smoking weed all the way. Back then, everybody thought the lead guitarist Eric Clapton was god.

Before he knew it, the set by Shady Grove was over. Victor straightened up and waited. The first of the group he was selling the dope to came into the club. There were two others with him. One Victor knew and the other was an unfamiliar woman. He was going to have to risk it. The three caught Victor's eye and he waved them over. When the waitress came, they ordered beers. Victor had another Coke. The hashish was in a small ammo bag. He took it off his shoulder and set it on the table. The buyer Victor knew best sat next to him. After casually placing the cash for the kilos in Victor's coat pocket, he picked up the ammo bag and stuck his hand inside, peeled away the foil and used his thumbnail to scrape a flake of hashish off the brick. Once that was done he brought his thumb to his nose, sniffed, and nodded. Meanwhile, Victor discreetly counted the money. The buyers sat back and enjoyed their beers and the first couple songs of the next band, which turned out to be GURUGURU. Victor loved this group, who were known for playing good driving German rock. The deal had gone down smooth as silk. He relaxed.. While he sat in the back of the club and nodded his head to the music Ana came in through the door. She looked around, found him and snuck into the seat next to him.

"Victor," she whispered in his ear and kissed it. "Allo."

Victor opened his eyes and smiled. What a pleasant surprise. He kissed her full on the mouth. She looked rosy in the lights reflecting off the stage.

"Hi. What brings you here?"

"I want to see you," smiled Ana. "It is Christmas tomorrow and we don't go to church so we come here. My mother tell me to spend Weihnachtsabend mit meinem Freund. I oblige."

"I'm glad you did." She sat on his lap for a few minutes and then moved to the chair next to Victor. He guessed that he would be putting off his return to the commune for a little while.

Victor walked out of the Red Star and heard a female calling his name. Looking around, he saw it was a young black woman. According to Ana, this was who her friend Porgy was hanging out with. Ana had pointed her out to him a week ago. Cute fuckin' girl. She was coming up the U-Bahn steps on the same side of the street as the commune. That's when she hollered Victor's name. He guessed Porgy had pointed him out to her at one of the few meetings on Angela he had attended or perhaps at a show where Porgy and his band played. He remembered them together at a GURUGURU show at the university. It was a fundraiser for the Angela committee. The girl introduced herself and started talking a mile a minute.

"Hi Victor you don't know me but my name is Martha and I see you at meetings and stuff and Porgy told me a little about you." She barely stopped for a breath. "I know your situation and just wanted to say that I think it's cool."

They were walking down Eschersheimer Landstrasse away from the PX. Fast. Victor smiled at her and put his hand on her shoulder to slow her down a little. She responded, walking a little slower. The sun reflected off the bright white stucco of the apartment buildings along the sidewalk.

"I just wanted to get away from the PX," she explained. "My mom and some of her friends are supposed to be meeting there for some Christmas shopping and I didn't want any of them to see me talking with somebody from the commune. Especially you 'cause if they saw me they might get the fuckin' MPs down on you all."

"Thanks." Victor said. "I appreciate that. You wanna' go get some coffee or somethin'?"

"Yeah. Sure." Martha followed him to a small coffee shop he occasionally hung out at. They sat down and ordered a pot of their strongest. Martha reached into her purse to pay.

"That's okay,."said Victor. "I'm cool. I can pay. So, how do you know Porgy? Are you in school or what's your deal?"

"Yeah. I'm a senior." She smiled. When she did her face radiated something special. One could tell she was a well-loved girl. Her hair was in braids, was quite thick and looked like it was a little hard to tame. She wore a beret á la the Black Panthers and had several political buttons pinned to the strap on her purse. Free Huey. End the War Now. Amis raus aus Vietnam. A couple Moratorium pins. Free Bobby and Ericka. On her jacket was a Free Angela pin with the famous picture of Angela.

"I wish I was through so I could do more political stuff, but I got a few more months. That's how I met Porgy—through political stuff last summer." She was talking about the Ramstein Two case.

"I've seen that band you and Porgy are in." He sipped on his coffee. It was quite hot. "You guys kick out some serious stuff."

"Thanks," she smiled shyly. "I love doing that. The music is fun to make and I feel like we're reaching people with our message, you know? Plus I get to do something with Porgy."

"You like the man, don't you?" Asked Victor. "I mean, you don't have to say anything but it's pretty apparent." Victor didn't know Porgy very well. Mostly what he knew he had heard from Ana, who seemed to respect him and let on that she found him attractive.

"I think I love him." She blushed, temporarily turning her beautiful brown skin a darker shade. "I don't think he knows it, though. It's like 'cause I'm in high school he doesn't want to mess with me."

Victor smiled and wondered what his thoughts would be if he were in Porgy's place. If anything, Porgy stayed away because her daddy was an officer who was super protective of his daughter. "You guys will figure it out, if it's meant to be."

"I hope so," said Martha. "My mom knows about

my feelings and she just said that the Lord takes care of things. I pointed Porgy out to her one time at the commissary. He was in the parking lot waiting for some lifer he was driving around. All she said was that he was a good looking man. I just agreed."

"Having your mom on your side is half the battle." Victor joked, trying to make light of the subject.

"I guess." Martha poured the rest of the coffee from the pot into her cup. "I better go. I'm supposed to meet my mom in a little while. I saw you and just wanted to meet you."

They finished their coffee and left the coffee shop. Victor headed south towards downtown Frankfurt and Martha headed north back towards the PX. He wondered if she would have looked for him in the Roter Stern if she hadn't run into him. He had to admit that he was surprised when she ran up to him but she's gotta' be cool. If he had the chance, Victor figured he would mention the meeting to Porgy. He rarely saw him even though he and Ana were pretty good friends. Victor continued south on Eschenheimer Landstrasse. He hoped to buy a little something to give Ana for Christmas

While I walked and shopped, a picture of my mom came into my head. It was from when me, her and Dad all lived together. Her blue eyes framed by her long straight black hair. I remember her thin frame that my buddies thought was sexy. She and I spent a lot of time together while Dad was driving coast-to-

coast. Our little house was sparsely decorated but I always felt rich with Mom around. She didn't work until after Dad died in that fuckin' accident. In fact, most of my friends' moms didn't work. Every day that it rained she would pick me up after school and we would go get an ice cream or go to the shopping center and get a treat. When Dad came home between runs it was like a holiday at the house. Even the dog and cat knew something good was going on.

Chicken dinners and helping her make French fries in the deep fryer. Walking Betsy the dog and playing in the yard. Setting up in Dad's truck and pretending we were going on a long trip. He was supposed to get a new cab that all three of us could fit comfortably in and we were all going to go with him on his runs during the summer. I was ten when the fuckin' brakes failed on his truck and he went off the road somewhere in Iowa. I was spared the details but it didn't matter 'cause all I knew was that he was dead. Mom freaked out. She didn't hear about it until three days after the accident then she cried and cried for days or weeks even. People came over at first to help but eventually they all went back to their own lives. Mom quit drinking beer and started in on Canadian whiskey. She was buying it by the half gallon. Uncle Jack came and checked in every once in a while and threw away all the whiskey whenever he visited. Mom had got some kind of settlement from the company that Dad drove for or from the truck manufacturer and didn't have to worry about money so she just bought more. Drinking and crying is all I remember of our last year together. I mostly stayed in my room and watched TV when I wasn't at school. Mom started going out at night 'cause I guess she was lonely. The day I turned eleven she meant to bake me a cake and make a special dinner but didn't wake up almost the whole fucking day. When I got home from school there was some dude arguing with her in the kitchen about buying the wrong kind of beer or something stupid like that. I stood outside the door and listened. She told him to go to hell. Then he slapped her. I came in then 'cause I wanted to kill the motherfucker. He looked at me with what I know now was total hatred. Then he left, calling her a bitch on the way out. She saw me and began to cry. Then she hugged me and cried and cried for what seemed like forever. Eventually, she cleaned herself up and said she was going to take me out to dinner for my birthday. When she asked me what I wanted I said I wanted her to quit drinking. She did. For about six months. Then I guess shit just got too much for her and she started up again, only she hid it from me. The men still came over though. Not the same asshole that hit her but other guys. Some of them were nice but most of them just wanted to fuck and didn't want me around. One day after she hadn't been home for a couple days Uncle Jack came and got me. He eventually worked it out with the courts to be my guardian. I would see

Mom every few days and hang out with her but that relationship we had when Dad was alive was gone forever. Last time I saw her was at high school graduation. I guess she just never recovered from losing Dad. If I ever get back to the world maybe we can reconcile some. If she's even alive.

Ana

I was with my mother. She asked me about Victor. I do not remember that she met him, but she said she did. I think it might be her imagination. I have talked about him when we are together. Her mind is not present many times when I see her. She thinks I am another person sometimes when I visit. That began when Papa died. She is not that old, but I think I might have to move her to another place for her own safety. But until she wants to go I cannot make her do that. She must have some dignity. We celebrated Christmas today. I brought her a gift that she opened and set on her table. It was a little Engel made from glass. Then we drank some wine and ate some Wurst mit Kraut. That is my mother's favorite meal. We talked for a little while and then she fell asleep. While she slept, I listened to the radio. The Hessischer Rundfunk was playing Debussy. It was good for my spirit. Debussy makes me calm. Then she woke up.

I made her a small dinner and waited until she went to bed. Then I took the Strassenbahn back to here. I am waiting for Victor to return. I wonder if he did meet my mother. We are going to the cinema again. We both like the privacy that we find in the dark. Here in Roter Stern there is not so much privacy. Always a meeting. Always the music and always the people talking and smoking and drinking. I like the motion but I want the quiet sometimes. I think Victor is the same. He made another hashish sale and is happy to have money. He says he likes to spend money on me. I told him I do not care. Maybe it is an American thing? Boys spend money on their girlfriends?

Mutti told me more about her life with Papa after they left the refugee camp. It was hard to find an apartment. That is why when they found the one on Kirschbaumweg, they never left it. They never had more children she said because they were afraid another war would come and they did not want to bring more Kinder into such a world. So we gave you all the love we had for all the Kinder we didn't have, she said. I almost cried when she said that. They always were full of much love for me. I never felt sad except when Papa died. When I cried he would tell me that the eyes were the fountain springs of the heart. He took me for walks along the river almost every day after he came home from the Fabrik near our house. We ice skated when the river was frozen. On Sundays, the three of us would ride the Strassenbahn into Frankfurt and walk around downtown. Then we would eat pommes frites and Kurrywurst at a Trinkhalle. After Papa bought an auto, we would drive up to the Taunus Mountains and walk on the trails there. When I begin to go to political meetings in gymnasium, my Papa said it was a good thing. You and your friends must stop the world from making another Hitler he said. Your Mutti and I have failed. We did not stop the evil. We pretended that things were not as bad as they were. That must never happen again. I wish I could have promised him it would not.

I think Victor is coming up the stairs.

Porgy

Martha told me she had coffee with Victor. I was surprised. I did point him out a time or two but didn't think she'd remember the cat. That girl's got some memory. When I asked her what they talked about all she said was not much. She'll tell me if she wants. I should talk to him soon, mostly 'cause Ana's been askin' I guess I'll do it even if it goes against my personal interests. That's the right thing to do. I wanna' make sure he ain't into somethin' he can't control beyond what he's already into. Ana seemed pretty good the other day. I'm thinkin' during the holidays they spent a lot of time together, which had to be a good thing. No meetings and no rallies or marches frees up one's time, if you know what I mean. I wish she could get him into something besides dope. Lots of brothers and white boys, especially ones in the fuckin' military, just wanna' empty their heads. Can't say I blame 'em. That's how I was in Nam but not like some of those motherfuckers who be smoking the heroin in their cigarettes and shit. I mean they was noddin' on guard duty and in formation. The lifers was drunk so nobody gave a flyin' fuck since the whole war was a pile of shit and by the time I was there wasn't hardly nobody pretending anything different.

I reckon Victor's been on the run now for almost six months. Either he's slick or invisible 'cause he ain't done much different since the day he showed up in Frankfurt.. I know where to find the motherfucker any day and I ain't even lookin'. Makes me think the pigs are lookin' the other way. I hear he been hanging with a couple shady cats down at Zoom Club. I mean the kind of cats who turn on you or turn you in for a shot of smack if you know what I'm sayin'. That's the shit that makes me nervous. One thing any ghetto child know is you can't trust a junkie. Not that I'm a ghetto child but I know the culture. Who's that writer? You know, the beatnik that wrote that Naked Lunch? That book he wrote about his junk days is revealing as hell about a junkie's priorities. He says that there ain't but one priority for a junkie. I guess I'll catch up with Victor some night down there soon. When I was a kid the preacher always said there was people who made things happen and there was ones who let things happen to them. I don't know which category Victor falls into, but I want to find out for Ana's sake. It'ain't really my place to say but she can't let her love blind her. If he fucks it up though, I'd pick up with that girl anytime .

Victor

Victor sat at his usual table in the back of the Zoom Club. It was early evening. 1972 was barely two weeks old. Shit was definitely heating up.

I stopped in at a meeting to wait for Ana last night. There must have been a hundred people in the room. It was at the university and was about Angela. People are getting into gear now that they know her sister Fania is definitely coming to Frankfurt in a few weeks. Angela herself is still working on her defense and sitting in prison. I have a feeling that as long as the pressure stays on the courts from the masses that her lawyers will find a way to get her out on bail. Then it's just a question of whether or not she sticks around. I don't know what I would do. I would probably run as quickly as I could. They played that Sweet Black Angel song by the Stones at the end of the meeting. It's pretty cool. Both the Stones and John and Yoko singing a song for her. I'm hoping some of the money from those songs is going to her defense. Anyhow, there's been two big busts outside Zoom the last week. Each one took down a few dozen keys of

Porgy walked into the club. He looked around, said hello to a couple black guys he knew and went to get a soda. The place smelled like hashish. Very good hashish. The last time he had been there was a benefit for the *Voice of the Lumpen* newspaper. Just a few German rock bands and a lot of speeches. The cool part happened after the club closed. Some of the musicians had stuck around and started jamming. Jazz players joined them from a club a few blocks over and it turned into a session that lasted until breakfast. Wine was the preferred intoxicant that time. He paid for his soda and caught Victor's eye at a table in the back. Victor waved and Porgy headed to his table.

"Hey," said Victor as he extended his hand, "Porgy, right? I've seen you around."

"Yeah. I seen you too," Porgy sat down opposite Victor. Nothing was said while they sipped their drinks. "Ana talks about you a lot."

"Cool," responded Victor. He told Porgy, "She has a lot of respect for you. Says you're one of the smartest guys she's ever met."

"That's a compliment." Porgy relaxed, leaning back

on his chair. "I would have to say something pretty similar about her. She is one smart lady."

"Ain't that the truth," agreed Victor. "Sometimes I wonder how I ended up being with her. I do learn a lot, though."

"Don't underestimate yourself, brother." Porgy grinned. To be honest, he wondered that himself sometimes, but there was no accounting for love.

A couple roadies were on the small stage at the other end of the club. Screeches and other types of feedback erupted in the hall. Porgy turned around for a minute.

"The music should be starting in a half hour or so." Victor stood up. "Do you want something more to drink?" Porgy shook his head no.

"I'll be back." Victor headed toward the bar. When he returned Porgy had switched seats so that he could see the stage.

"Who is this band that's coming up?" asked Porgy.

"I'm not sure, but it's got a couple British blues guys in it that played with Mayall and Clapton. You gonna' stick around?"

"Yeah," answered Porgy. "Why the hell not?"

Victor was preparing a small chunk of hashish. Once he had softened it with a flame and crumbled it into a small pipe he carried around, he fired it up and passed it to Porgy. Porgy took a hit and passed it back.

"Nice pipe," noted Porgy.

"Ana gave it to me." Victor took a big hit and

passed it back. Porgy shook his head no.

"I'm good, man," he explained, "I don't smoke that much."

Victor nodded and extinguished the ember. The two men quietly enjoyed the effects of the smoke. The tables in the club were beginning to fill up. Soon there would be only standing room. A group of German gymnasium students sat near Porgy and Victor. Emboldened by a few beers, they laughed loudly and talked about their school day adventures. Victor understood most of what they were saying. Hanging out with Ana and almost exclusively with Germans had improved his comprehension tremendously. One of the girls in the group recognized Porgy and walked over to the table.

"Allo," she smiled. "You are from the Angela Davis committee, ja?"

Porgy nodded yes. The girl sat down. "I have not been to a meeting for a Monat...a month. What is going on mit Angela Davis?"

"Her sister kommt nach Frankfurt," said Porgy. "Next meeting is Donnerstag at the Jugendzentrum neben der Hausbesetzung called Che Guevara Haus. Um 19:30."

"Danke," she shook Porgy's hand, nodded to Victor and returned to her friends.

"Doesn't that make you a little nervous?" asked Victor. "People recognizing you like that?"

"Part of the deal, man," Porgy said softly. "At least

I know people are paying attention."

"Yeah. I guess."

"What about you, man?" asked Porgy. "Do you ever get nervous? Your situation is a lot more illegal than mine. Fuck, the wrong people see you, you're a goner."

"I've been laying low ever since that bust outside of here a few days ago. It's been getting hot around the clubs." Victor looked at Porgy. He wondered how obvious his dealing gig was. "Gotta' figure out another way to make some cash if I quit dealing though. Or I could go to Sweden I guess. I don't wanna' leave Ana though."

"Just be careful who you talk with is all, man." The band members were taking their places on the small stage. Soon it would be too loud to talk. The waitress came around and each man ordered another soda.

"I know, man."

Here we are. Waiting in line for the Tull show. Ana right next to me. I feel really good. Not just because I'm buzzed but in general. Roter Stern had a big party a few days ago and it really helped lighten some of the heavy shit people been feeling with rumors of busts and cops and narcs and all that shit. People put their stereo in the window and blasted music into the courtyard. There was all kinds of food, all kinds of drink, all kinds of hash and acid and we just let it loose. There must have been a couple hundred freaks partying and generally enjoying themselves. It started around noon and we brought it indoors around eight in the evening to keep the pigs away. While we were hanging out inside, people started reminiscing about the early days of the Hausbesetzung movement. It wasn't long after some big battle they call the battle of Grunebergweg that the Hausbesetzung thing really got moving. Apparently, from what I could understand of the conversation, people took over some fancy house on that street back in 1971. Turned out that the estate or whatever was owned by some Iranian friend of the Shah who was also a friend of some bigwigs in Frankfurt politics so they demanded the cops take it back. It was one hell of a fight. The thing is, even though the cops won the building back they lost the support of the respectable citizens and most of City Hall. That opened up the current big wave of squatting that Roter Stern was part of. It was certainly something to celebrate. After the music died down, Ana and I loved each other until we passed out

.

There's lots of cops around the concert hall. Dogs and everything. Reminds me of the Stones show last year. Their presence doesn't seem to change anything. People are still drinking and smoking. Dealers are still selling hash and whatever. The weather could be better but at least the rain slowed down to a drizzle. It will be nice to get inside where it's warm. Ana is snuggling close. I told her she should wear more clothes but she just said she would lose them inside once she got warm. So she's wrapping herself around me. I'm not complaining mind you. Just sayin'. My hair is gettin' pretty long which helps me stay warm. I think it's longer than ever. Uncle Jack never let me grow it out too much. He said it got in the way of the farm work. I didn't think it did but figured it wasn't worth arguing about. I still had some of the longest hair on a guy in that conservative little Indiana town. The school even tried to suspend me a couple times unless I cut it. So I just cut it.

Good. The crowd is moving toward the gates. Must be time to go in. Ana is shivering she's so cold. Just in time I guess. There's some friends of hers. Looks like they're passing out leaflets. I wonder if it's for Angela or the squats. That whole issue has been heating up, too. The city is getting a lot of pressure from the housing speculators again to clear out the Westend. I tell you when that happens it will be one hell of a fuckin' battle. Those people got their shit together. Their defenses will not fall easily. I just hope no one gets killed when it goes down. On either side. The fuckin' cops don't know what they are up against. Hell, it's those people's home so I can't say I blame 'em. Still though, it's some serious shit. Cool, the line is moving. Here we go!

Once inside, Ana and Victor wandered around the

perimeter of the Festhalle floor. The building was part of a fairgrounds complex and was used for everything from rock concerts to the Frankfurt Book Fair. Bicycle races also took place there. Three different Strassen-bahns stopped out front. The northern entrance to the autobahn was five hundred meters away.

After buying a beer to share and inching their way to a space about forty feet from the stage, Victor and Ana sat down. Victor took out a chunk of hash and a pipe and fired up a bowl. He had taken some acid earlier. After tripping the day before he knew that the acid wouldn't do much more than keep him awake. Tolerance with LSD built up fast. Ana did not want to trip so she was depending on the music to keep her going.

The floor of the Festhalle was full. People wan-dered around looking for seats in the balcony that surrounded three of the four walls. She was really looking forward to Gentle Giant. Some of that band's members were on stage tuning their instruments. The room had warmed up considerably. Victor removed his coat and set it on the floor. Ana moved her body onto it. She smiled at Victor and kissed him. The lights went down and the crowd erupted in applause and cheers.

"Dieser Abend," began the announcer. "Lippmann und Rau bringen von England...Gentle Giant und die Grosse Gruppe Jethro Tull!" Gentle Giant was on stage. The opening notes of their tune "The Giant" began. Ana stood up. The sound of the organ slowly filled the hall. Then came the rest of the band. Victor re-lit the pipe of hashish and passed it to Ana. She smiled and smoked. Gentle Giant's music was mostly composed of longer melodies that were somewhat reminiscent of classical music only louder and more raucous. Which made sense, laughed Victor, since it was rock music. In what seemed like less than an hour to the two of them, but was probably closer to an hour and half, Gentle Giant's set came to an end. The lights came up slightly and Ana sat back down on Victor's coat. Victor went to find a bathroom while Ana remained in their spot. Upon Victor's return they smoked another pipe and shared it with those around them--mostly Germans but also a couple of GIs . The anticipation grew as the intermission stretched into a forty-five minute wait.

The lights went down. A spot shone down on Jethro Tull's Martin Barre, who held an acoustic guitar. The opening notes to "My God" emanated from the guitar. The crowd erupted. He began to sing and then the entire band joined in. From the side of the stage, Ian Anderson walked into the light playing his flute. He wore his trademark overcoat like the character from his song Aqualung. The next tune was "Thick As a Brick." About two hours later, Victor and Ana left as happy as clams.

Ana

It has been a good time since before Christmas. The political meetings have been replaced with more festive happenings. Although I like political meetings, it is nice to have a break. We have had only two small meetings for Angela. We have the date for her sister's visit to Frankfurt. There was one big meeting über die Häuserkampf. A member of the bourgeois citizens group from Westend expressed their support. They donated money for the Jugendzentrum. Victor and I have made very much love. I am glad that I take birth control otherwise I could get pregnant with all the lovemaking. There was a party at Roter Stern. Everyone cooked something and brought it to the courtyard. We ate and danced and smoked and drank. Victor said he never wanted it to end. He is so Americanisch. He just always wants to have a good time. We went to the Gentle Giant and Jethro Tull concert which was the best concert I think I have ever attended. Now it is time to be seriously working. There are meetings every night. I hope that Victor does not become upset because I am busy.

Victor

The night was incredibly cloudy. Even with all of the streetlights in the Hauptbahnhof area, it still seemed dark. Victor walked through a back alley that led to a back entrance to the Zoom Club. It had been at least a week since he had been inside. The Tull concert from two nights previous was still fresh in his mind. He figured that it was time to get back into business. It had been almost a month since he made his last purchase or sale. He was scheduled to meet a friend of Tarachi's in the back room tonight. Just for a taste. Apparently there was something new around. Well, new to the Frankfurt market anyhow. Instead of the red hashish, this new stuff was supposed to be black on the outside and a dark lush green on the inside. Supposedly, it was even stronger than the red although not as harsh. Victor was supposed to get a few grams tonight to smoke and spread around. If people liked it he was going to buy a few kilos of the shit.

He was sober. No alcohol or drugs of any kind in his system. In fact, all he had drunk the entire day was some English breakfast tea with Ana before she headed off to her meeting. It was her third in the last two days, with things getting pretty intense on that front. Since Angela Davis's sister was due in town in a month, preparations were going into high gear. Ana was on the security committee as well as a couple others. In addition, the political debates were heating up around how much different groups were going to cooperate with the DKP and vice versa. The Revolutionärer Kampf people really didn't like the Moscow party people and the feeling was mutual. According to Ana, the differences were more than political and involved disagreements around culture and issues like drugs and rock music. Ana was friends with both groups and had taken it upon herself to charm them all into playing nice around the Free Angela struggle. She must be good at it, thought Victor. She certainly seemed to enjoy the intensity of the whole thing.

He was within a block of the Zoom Club's rear door. As he got closer he noticed at least four people in the alley on that block. Hesitant to move closer, he slowed down. Suddenly, a bunch of shouting erupted among the four. As far as Victor could tell, one man was yelling Polizei and struggling to pull something out of his jacket pocket--perhaps a gun. Victor wasn't sure. He ducked into a a doorway, crouched behind several tall trash bins and froze, afraid to even breathe. Catching occasional glimpses of the action in his line of sight, he saw a man get hit on the head and fall to the ground. Two other men immediately ran away from where Victor hid. Another man spoke in German into a radio and took off after the two men that had fled. While Victor stood both nervously and quietly in the doorway, he watched the other man get up and a police car pull into the alley with its lights off. One policeman got out of the passenger side, spoke with the man that had been knocked down and helped him find something he had dropped. He was definitely a cop. Then the two men got into the police car and drove down the alley towards Victor, who pulled himself as far into the shadows of the trash bins as possible. After the car passed, he waited five minutes, breathed a sigh of relief and left on foot. The entire scene he witnessed fueled him with enough adrenalin to walk all the way back to the commune.

Three more fuckin' busts around the Zoom Club since the Tull show. The cops must have been setting this shit up for a while. I've only been back once since the shit I saw go down in the alley that night. When I went into the club I heard all about that failed bust and three successful ones. Ana showed me in the Frankfurter Rundschau how the cops are making a big deal about it. Headlines even saying that they busted a big hashish ring. I never did get my taste and am getting pretty damn low on smoking goods. The management won't allow any smoking inside the club, not even tobacco. Pretty crazy. Their business is way off. Lucky for them they didn't have any big acts scheduled. A couple of the cats that were busted were GIs. I think one of 'em is a friend of McRice's from my old unit. If the CID wasn't in on the investigation before, you can be pretty sure they are now. Fuck. That makes my risk a little greater, I guess. I still haven't told Ana how close that whole scene was the other night. Plus, she's got more important shit going on.

My plan is to lay low for a little while longer and stay away from the Zoom Club until the heat cools. Tarachi should be back in the city in another week and he and I can put something together. I did hear about some microdot acid being available but I never really been into selling acid. Heroin is around but the negative karma on that is bad.

Ana

The rally is tonight. We have prepared as much as we possibly can. Fania Davis Jordan is already in Frankfurt. I met her last night. She is a beautiful woman in her features and her soul. She is very calm. I think she is truly afraid for her sister and is very thankful for all the support she has received. I think the rally will be a success.

I hope Victor comes. He has been a concern in recent days. I think he smokes too much hashish. He is very depressed. He asked me to get him out of the country. I do not know if he is a good person to help leave. This might be because I love him I cannot think about helping him desert. There is one part of me that believes he should leave. He must be getting the attention of the police. Everyone knows that the Zoom has police there every night. They look for drugs. When I think about him leaving, I get sad and scared. I am sad for me and scared for him. I think he could get to Sweden but I do not know how he would do in Stockholm. There has been some pressure on the deserter groups there from the US Embassy. There are rumors

Ana got off the number 13 Strassenbahn. She was at the Opernplatz. The hall where the rally was scheduled to be held was a few blocks away. There was a small rally going on in front of the bombed out opera building. Something about the Hausbesetzung. The police had still not raided any squats, but the rumors were growing more frequent. Most people involved figured the raids would be soon. The Roter Stern was probably safe for a while longer because of its location. Too close to the US installation and not in the actual Westend, the real estate it sat on was not valuable enough yet.

Ana waited for a traffic light to change. She looked at the Opernhaus. Whenever she saw the partially destroyed building she got upset. The Americans had bombed it back in the war even though it was not a military target. Meanwhile, they had left the IG Farben building standing. IG Farben, one of the biggest users of slave labor during the Nazi regime. The story was that the American generals wanted the building for their headquarters when they finally defeated the Nazis. Now it was the headquarters for several US military commands. The Opernhaus was a beautiful building at one time. One could still see its architecture and decorative sculptures in the part that remained. Once, when she was a teen, Ana and a few friends had snuck through the fencing that surrounded the building. They were drunk and high and wanted to see what was there. All they found were a few rats scurrying over dust and concrete. The place smelled like shit. The light changed and she crossed the street. She went back to thinking about Victor.

It was getting dark. The lights of the city were bright. As Ana approached the hall she looked for her comrades. They were supposed to let her in the back door by the stage. It was decided that she would begin by passing out leaflets at the front as people entered. Everyone involved in the organization of the rally was also supposed to watch the people in the crowd for any potential trouble. The Communist Party organizers had received threats from some right wing individuals warning of a bomb. Frankfurt's police had done a brief search of the building but they were not to be trusted. The party security men had spent most of the day looking around and guarding the building from unknown persons. After she and the others had taken their places, the building was opened and people began to enter. A sizable crowd had already gathered outside. At first, it was almost impossible to give everyone a leaflet that described the program. Ana saw Porgy and his music group get out of a car and enter through another door. They were second on the program, certain to be more interesting than all the speeches from the DKP communists.

A couple of Black Panthers from *The Voice of the Lumpen* began to sell their papers near her. One of them was the guy named Nkrumah. She struck up a conversation.

"Allo Nkrumah." She smiled his way. "Wie geht's?"

"Good sister," he answered. "Real good. Looks like we have a full house."

The edition was a special issue just for the rally with a headline about the struggle to free Angela coming to Europe. Nkrumah and his partner could not keep up with the demand for the papers. Like the Black Panther paper in the States, *The Voice of the Lumpen* was very popular.

"I think we will only have standing room," agreed Ana. Nkrumah nodded and gave her a quick power salute with his fist. He then got down to the business of selling papers. Ana heard a commotion outside the hall. She and a couple other organizers moved towards the door. The night was cold and when she stepped outside to check on the situation the breeze temporarily stung her eyes. The steps were crowded with people trying to get in. Meanwhile, a right-wing group of perhaps fifteen Germans were attempting to prevent people from getting to the doors. Ana spoke briefly with another organizer.

"I will go find the security group," she yelled across the crowd to her fellow organizer.

"Good idea," responded the other. "I'll watch

these fascists." The speaker was a swarthy black GI who boxed in amateur bouts on bases all over Europe. He walked down the steps toward the right-wingers. Ana went into the building and returned a few minutes later with three more big men. They joined the organizer already on the steps and formed a wedge that slowly but firmly pushed the right wing agitators away from the steps and down the sidewalk. The rally was scheduled to begin in ten minutes. It was time to urge the crowd to get inside. This was done with a megaphone. The speaker repeated his encouragement in German and English. By eight o'clock most of the crowd was inside the hall. There were hundreds standing in the back and on the sides of the room. The hall was above capacity. Ana went to the front of the hall. Her job was to stand in front of the stage and keep an eye out for trouble.

The rally began with a speech from the local leader of the DKP. He welcomed everybody and talked about the meaning of Angela's fight for freedom. He interspersed the politics with personal reminiscences from her time as a student at Goethe Universität. Apparently they knew each other back then. Then he talked about the anti-racist struggle and its role in the international battle against U.S. imperialism. He finished up with a suggestion that people think about joining the party. After that speaker's departure, Porgy and his musical group The Ghetto Poets set up their equipment with the help of some friends. While the audience waited, a recording of Angela speaking about the Soledad Brothers played over the loudspeaker. Twenty minutes later, The Ghetto Poets began. Their rhythms and chanting made most of the young people tap their feet and nod their heads to the drums. The older folk were less receptive. They played for thirty minutes. The show ended with Porgy and Martha singing a song that the group had written about Angela. Then there was silence. People left their seats to use the rest rooms and talk with friends and comrades. Newspaper sellers wandered around selling their papers. Ana gave away a couple hundred buttons that said Freiheit für Angela Davis. Then the lights blinked. People returned to their seats. There was much anticipation. A man from Revolutionärer Kampf approached the microphone. He greeted the crowd and spoke in German then English, introducing Fania Davis Jordan. The applause was very loud and lasted a while. Then Fania spoke. Several men, including three or four Black Panthers from the U.S. and Germany stood around her as protection while she spoke. She was an average size woman with beautiful features. Her voice was strong and her spirit was stronger. Ana saw Victor standing near the back of the balcony. That made her happy even though he did not wait for her afterward. He was afraid there were undercover policemen from the Army there.

Porgy

Shit. The gig went off really well. The old German cats were tapping their toes even though you know they didn't know the music at all. Fania tore the house down. Her speech about the situation around her sister and the racist pigs in the States got everyone on their feet. I'd guess about half of the crowd were Americans. Mostly brothers but some white GIs were there. So were some kids from the high school. A genuine success. Plus, as a bonus, me and Martha got it on. It was totally her lead. I told her after the leafleting at Edwards that I dug her but was a little scared off 'cause of her old man. After the rally we put our drums and stuff into the car. Then we went back inside for a little after-event party and summing up. She sat down in front of me on the floor and just moved her ass right into me. When there was a lull she asked do I want to leave with her. We split and went to a brother's apartment near Gruneberg Park -- some cat from Chicago who stayed overseas after getting out of the army. He had given Martha a key and we went in. The rest was fine, just fine. It's been a day or two and I ain't seen her..

Ana asked me to hang out with Victor again. She's concerned about him and his dopin'. Especially with the busts goin' down at that club. I told her I would. Some of the German cats who been knowin' Ana a lot longer than me say they ain't never seen her so hung up over a guy. Victor must be doing somethin' right but damned if I know what it is. It's scary to see how love can make people blind to a person's faults, especially pretty obvious ones. I think the cat needs to wake up and deal with his situation. It ain't that I'm hard or nothing but he's like a lot of cats -- especially white ones -- from the States. They think the world is against them and they act like babies. The fact is the world is against you but so fuckin' what. You gotta' fight back. You can't just hide in some dope or what-ever. I seen that all the time with my mom's church people. Don't worry, they say, the Lord'll take care of things. Or, that's the Lord's will child. Dope ain't no different. It's just takin' away the pretense of the Lord so you just go get high. So many brothers are in that place it's downright tragic. Now the white kids going to the same place 'cause they found out the world don't give a shit and that they got to fight to change it. Fightin' be hard man. Anyhow I'll go look up Victor and chill with him some. Oh yeah, Fania kicked ass. Her line went something like Angela Davis is not just one person called Angela Davis: she is a symbol. She is not just a problem of the United States, and it is the responsibility of us all, of the entire world, to save her. A couple solid sisters, those two.

I ran into some brothers from Höchst there. They got themselves a big fuckin' mess. A higher concentration of black men on that post than anywheres else in Germany and some genuine crackers running the place. This one colonel calls his Negro lifer henchman "boy", and the fuckin' dude just takes it. Who knows, maybe that colonel got something on the Tom that's lickin' his boots. Anyhow, that place is gonna' blow soon. That's what these brothers was tellin' me. Already, some white guy tried to burn down the colonel's office quonset but the fire didn't take. Everybody knows who did it but no one's been busted yet. The white guy who fired it been keepin' a low profile ever since. Seems he got tired of being pushed around by the lifers in the unit. According to the brothers, he hangs with 'em a lot and was gettin' called a nigger-lover and all that tired shit by some of the white lifers and some of the GIs. So he said fuck it I'm gonna' burn down the office. I tell ya' I'm expectin' some trouble out of there soon.

Martha

I can't believe how great the night was. It all just happened like I dreamed. Me and Porgy just came together like we was meant to be. The sex was beautiful. It's even better when you love the man you doin' it with. Not like I'm a very experienced woman, but I know just 'cause I know. The other cats I been with were mere children compared with Porgy. Funny how a few years can make a difference. Now I can say like that white girl Ellen said to me when she started seeing that older cat: I sleep with men now, not no boys.

Seeing Fania was another thing altogether. The sister love and the love for the people was all over her face and in her soul. I don't think I'm being too romantic about the political shit when I say that. Her and my first time with Porgy are gonna' be forever one in my being. I don't know if it can get better than that. I just wish Daddy wasn't such an asshole about protectin' me. Maybe he won't find out about Porgy. I think the political stuff is okay with Daddy, even though he ain't nothing but a liberal at best I think he understands that our generation gotta' take it further.

He'll give me a little crap about his fuckin' career and my politics but underneath that he'll be thinkin' how proud he is that he's got a child that cares about her people. It's the Porgy thing he ain't gonna' like if he finds out. I hope his fuckin' spies don't know.

When Fania said that bit about even if we get Angela free it not being the end of the struggle but the beginning, I thought I was gonna' fuckin' cry. Either that or go grab a gun. I think pretty much everyone in that building felt just like me. I'm at the library now hopin' to finish up some homework then I wanna' go to a meeting at the university. Porgy should be there unless he got held up by his CO. When I talked to him yesterday he said they were fuckin' with him. He wasn't sure why but like he said they didn't have to look far for a reason as far as they were concerned. I just wanna' feel his arms around me. I wonder if mama ever felt that way about daddy. She must have. It seems to me like they still love each other but it also seems like daddy be too wrapped up in being the officer to pay attention like maybe he used to. That's one thing I'm looking forward to about being in the States next year for college. I can talk to mama and daddy's people and try and find out what they really like. I mean I know they came from somewheres but I don't know hardly anything but the geography. We always moving so we never get to just be in with family. They always make a big deal about it when we show up for a holiday or something but then it's all about the holiday and making us all comfortable. You never hear the facts that way. Just the pretty memories and talk. I don't want dirt but I do want truth. It's like they the golden children and nobody remembers anything bad that happened to 'em or that they might have done.

I should get back to this homework- another paper for English. We're reading Invisible Man, appropriately enough. I hope Porgy shows up here. He knows I'm at the library.

No sooner had Martha said this to herself when Porgy came through the door. He walked over to the magazine section and grabbed the copy of *Rolling Stone*. It was a white guy's magazine for the most part but he liked their writing and his musical tastes were pretty universal. He looked around for Martha, spotted her and headed over to the table where she sat. After sitting down next to her, she kissed him full on the mouth. The librarian watched and looked away when he saw Porgy looking right at him. Porgy was just a little nervous but naturally couldn't resist kissing her back. After saying hello, Martha went back to her homework and Porgy read his magazine. Twenty minutes passed like this, then Martha began putting away her books.

"Let's go into the park," she suggested. Gruneburg Park was mcrc yards away from the back of the library building. Porgy helped her pack up her belongings and the two of them left the building. Once outside, Martha grabbed his hands, pushed her body against his and kissed. They headed to the park. Once they were situated under a tree in a relatively hidden space, they kissed some more.

Porgy stopped. "Is your father pissed at you?" He almost felt like a teenager asking the question. The reality was that he didn't want to get his ass in too much trouble. The years between the two were only three or four but in the strange world of the military, sometimes that could be the same as twenty when it came to officers' kids and GIs. Martha's old man was known for being a hard ass. If Porgy was to be generous he might say that was the only way a black man could get as far as her old man had in Uncle Sam's army. However, generous was not the mood Porgy was in. He just didn't want to end up on some assignment that was worse than the one he had. He kept on flashing to the story in the bible where King David sends Uriah to battle because he wanted his wife Bathsheba. Of course, the circumstances were different and the old man didn't have that kind of power, but he could make Porgy's life hell until his discharge.

"I don't care whether he's pissed or not," said Martha. "I really don't."

"I gotta' be careful," warned Porgy. "He could make my life damn uncomfortable if he didn't want me hanging out with you. I only got seven more months left in the army and I wanna' go out without a lot of shit on me."

"But I love you." Martha rubbed Porgy's thigh. He stiffened.

"I hear ya'. We just gotta' be careful. Especially with all this political shit we involved in. Don't you think that's the most important?"

"Yeah," agreed Martha. "You're right. Still, I wanna' see you no matter what my dad fuckin' says."

"We'll figure it out, babe." Martha moved onto Porgy's lap and kissed Porgy deeply. They left the park and headed toward the apartment where they had first made love.

Fire/Passion

Porgy and Ana were in the Hot Times bar. The momentum from the rally was still fresh. Its energy had propelled them both for at least a week. Fania was almost through with her European tour and her Frankfurt stop had been one of the highlights. The momentum in the California courtroom where Angela was on trial was leaning her way. Porgy and Ana were well into their third beer of the afternoon. It was time to sum things up and relax a bit. Porgy told Ana about the conversation with the GIs from Höchst. The morning news had mentioned several vehicles in the motor pool compound there being scorched. Porgy had a feeling that the fire had something to do with the conversation he had had.

"I think it is a good thing." Said Ana. "The pigs need to know that they cannot keep acting like they do."

Porgy nodded. "I guess I agree. I just hate to see them get busted for shit like this, though. They'll get put away for a long fuckin' time."

"Maybe we can discover who it is and I can help them leave." Suggested Ana.

"If they want to leave."

"Ja. If they want to." Agreed Ana. She watched as the German police harassed a young man outside the bar. After a few minutes of heated conversation between the police and the young man, the police continued walking down the street. The young man walked quickly away in the opposite direction. The sky, which had been bright and sunny, was turning gray. It was looking like rain. Porgy and Ana drank one more beer and left. After leaving the bar, both walked toward the Hauptbahnhof to catch the U-Bahn. As they walked Porgy put his arm around Ana's waist. She responded in kind, pulling him close. Without speaking, they boarded the U-Bahn and got off at the stop near the PX and Roter Stern.

Not sure what they would find, but driven by a repressed desire and a need to express what both had been leaving unsaid, they headed into the commune and up to the room Ana shared with Victor. It was empty. Porgy leaned down and kissed Ana long and hard. She responded with equal passion, closing the door to the room and leading Porgy to the mattress. A few short moments later they were naked. Porgy began to kiss her again. Ana reached behind his back and ran her fingers along his spine. Their lust took over. Even if Victor had shown up, it would not have mattered. When they were finally fulfilled, Porgy sat up and begin putting his clothes back on. Ana kissed his chest.

"I did not think that would happen," she whispered.

"I should say that I wish it didn't, " said Porgy. "But that would be a lie."

Ana smiled. It would be a lie for her, too. She began to pull on her clothing. Although she thought she should say something more, she didn't. Neither did Porgy. Once dressed, they left the commune for another beer.

The next morning, there was a small article in the *Stars & Stripes* newspaper about the firebombings. The article downplayed the damage and also mentioned a previous attempt to burn down the officers quonset hut. It concluded by stating that the military Criminal Investigation Division and an agency of the German Bundespolizei were investigating the incident.

Porgy

So that cat who was talking with me at the rally finds me in the library. I'm thinkin' 'bout Ana and waiting for Martha when he comes up and starts rappin' to me about the shit that went down in Höchst around the jeeps and shit. I tell him to hold it down. After all, we was on military property. I'm not sure about the cat anyway, if you know what I mean. He could be a cop or he could just be crazy. Either way I aim to be careful. We leave the library and go to Gruneburg Park. So he starts talkin'.

"Man we was all up getting high and shit. Then that white cat I tol' you about. The one who set the fire to the man's hut? He starts talkin' about how he figured out how to blow up a bunch of jeeps all at once. Talking about getting some fuse and tying some half-empty toilet paper rolls soaked in gas on them. Spacing the rolls out so they can be stuck in each gas tank of a row of jeeps. Then lighting the fuse and watching them blow. He works at the motor pool. We don't say nothing 'cause some of the brothers don't trust the cat with him being white and all. Me, I just think he's a bit of a firebug not that that can't be useful but shit.... Anyhow, I walk out of the barracks 'cause I don't want to be involved right yet. I mean, if they do it fine by me but I don't want my name on this thing 'cause it's got too many risks in it. So I head over to this off-base apartment where a brother lives with his girlfriend. I hang there a couple days 'cause I'm on leave anyhow. When I go back to work a couple days later I see CID motherfuckers and MPs everywhere. They checkin' everyone's ID and putting brothers and hippie GIs up against the wall. I check my pockets to make sure I ain't got anything incriminatin' on me and walk to the gate. Sho' 'nuf they put me up against the wall and frisk me. I take offense at this white motherfucker CID guy slammin' on my balls and push him down. Next thing I know there's four MPs on me--all white ones. I fight 'em off and take off runnin'. I been hidin' out for three days now and I got to figure out what to do. I seen you comin' onto the library from where I been sleepin' in this park and figured you might could help me."

"Bro," said Porgy. "Let's get away from the base. I ain't sure how I can help you other than gettin' you some food and other clothes, but let's see what we can get together."

Porgy figured he could find Ana or another radical friend with connections in the besetzenden Häuser and get the fellow into one of the squats for a few days; at least until they figured out whether or not he wanted to go to Sweden. He seemed genuine, but it was up to Ana and her group to decide if he was. The two men walked through the park away from the library. Until he spoke with someone in the squats, Porgy knew a place where a couple friends recently out of the service lived with their girlfriends. This guy could get some food and clothes and begin making plans there. He gave up the idea of hanging out with Martha.

Ana

Victor has been out very much lately. I heard that there have been many arrests at the Zoom Club. I do not know if he is selling hashish but when he is here he only sleeps. We have made love only three times since the rally. I have not been so busy but he has not been around to have sex with. I hope he is not doing heroin but I do not know what to think. There are six or seven people living at Roter Stern that we think are using and maybe selling heroin. There is talk about making them leave. I think they should be challenged first. That is fair. Two besetzende Häusen were busted by the Polizei because of heroin. They were not political houses but they are part of the collective and need to be strong. There is no place for drugs like that. But now, rock bands romanticize heroin and cocaine and the hippies think it is okay. The Black Panthers know better. They say it is like a chain that makes you a slave. If Victor is one of those using, then I must find out. I do not want him to be thrown out of the commune.

This evening while I sit here and listen to Anthem

of the Sun, the Grateful Dead album Victor has given me, I hope all is okay. Porgy has just left. He brought some leaflets for a meeting about Angela. There is a big conference we will call Am Beispiel der Angela Davis. It will be in Frankfurt in June. If she is free we will try and have her speak. If she is still in prison I think it will be a very large riot against the American Konsulat. Porgy and I talked about the war in Vietnam and about Victor. He said he thinks Victor may be what you say, over his head in something? I asked what that means. Porgy said it means he might be involved with things and people he does not understand and cannot control. I asked Porgy if he could help. He said he will try but I think he is hesitant. After all, we just made love again for a third time. His feelings for me might affect what he tells Victor, although I do not think he is the jealous kind. I have to be honest, I try not to have sex with Porgy, but I do believe in free love and don't see why I should limit my sex life to Victor. It is a struggle between what we are told about romance all through childhood and the reality of having feelings for more than one person. Of course, Victor doesn't know but I would tell him if he asked.

Porgy also talked about a GI from Höchst that approached him about maybe leaving the country. The GI is maybe one of the people that tried to burn military cars in protest. I think the act was good in that instance. I will try to meet with him and discuss.

It will be hard to convince the rest of the group I work with in the deserter project. They are all Pazifisten and do not like violence to anybody or anything. Porgy said that he will help me however he can. Perhaps we will have to help this man ourselves? I think I hear Victor coming to the room. I think if I had to choose one man I would choose Victor.

The Colonel

"You will not be seeing that young man again. That means no music rehearsals, no dates, nothing but school and church." Martha's father was angry. He was rehearsing the talk he planned on giving her that evening. It was not something he looked forward to. Although he loved his daughter, he sometimes wished he had six boys instead. He understood how guys thought. Girls, and women for that matter, were a different story.

His secretary Ursula had seen Martha with that troublemaker at a movie downtown when Martha should have been in school. It was one thing to date the guy, but to skip school to see him was beyond what he could allow. The Colonel just didn't get it. He had worked his ass off and swallowed a lot of pride to get this far in the man's army. Apparently, so had the father of this fellow Martha was swooning over. The Colonel had done his homework and checked personnel files of both the boy and his father. The father, Chief Master Sergeant Johnson, was one of those NCOs that stood out in the army. A Negro that the colonel liked to say acted like Jackie Robinson for the betterment of the race. Kept his mouth shut even when the racists were trying their best to make him strike out. The colonel could relate to that situation. After all, that was also his strategy. There had been plenty of times when he felt like punching a cracker who was riding him. This Porgy fellow seemed to have started in the military the same as his dad. Even though the reports the colonel had read hinted that Porgy was never interested in a military career, he had kept his mouth shut in boot camp. Even while he was in Vietnam, he was primarily a good soldier. Then something cracked and he was written up three times in two months; one marijuana write-up and two politically charged events. Of course, the political events had to do with black power issues. However, since he had been in Germany Porgy's record was clean. CID had notes about his involvement in activities involving the Black Panther Party and their causes, but it didn't seem to affect his work. He had nothing but excellent ratings. It probably helped that his current CO was a northerner known for his liberal views. If he had ended up with the far more typical southerner, he would be in the stockade along with his militant friends.

It's not like the Colonel couldn't appreciate the anger. What he didn't get was that these youngsters--and that's what they were--had it so much better than the Colonel and his generation did. Outright segregation was illegal. Negroes could legally get a job wherever they wanted. He knew that wasn't the case in practical terms, but the fact that white men couldn't call him boy and get away with it made the Colonel smile. Hell, some of them even had to salute him. Yeah, he got the anger but not the rest of it. It was the communism and so on that really bothered him. He thought they should all read that book, *Invisible Man*. Now that was the history of the Negro in the United States. Everybody was always trying to use the Negro for their own cause or entertainment. Nobody except for the black people themselves really had the fate of the Negro in mind. Even some of them could not be trusted.

The Colonel sat down at his desk and sipped his cup of coffee. Discovering it had turned cold, he asked his secretary to fix him a warm cup. After she set the fresh cup on his desk and left, he took a copy of the *Overseas Weekly* from his briefcase. Although the paper was frowned on by official military, it was considered essential reading by most officers and older NCOs just as a means of staying somewhat in touch with the enlisted men. Jokingly called the Oversexed Weekly by most folks because each issue usually included a few photographs of topless women, the tabloid played up racial and other troubles in the service while also highlighting German merchants and landlords that discriminated against GIs because of their skin color or just because they were GIs. A recent series had highlighted a simmering conflict on the Höchst Kaserne regarding an unenlightened officer and his treatment of the enlisted men under his command. The series had put the officer in a negative spotlight and from all reports the Colonel was hearing, the reports had only made him more of a jerk than before. Accused of openly racist taunts against black soldiers and unnecessary harassment of white enlisted men that didn't go along with the officer's prejudices, his actions were getting the notice of people all the way up to the Pentagon. As he sipped his coffee, the Colonel read about a firebomb attack on the Höchst Kaserne's motor pool. No one was hurt and there was very little damage but tensions had been raised with some dependents in the adjoining housing area joining in on both sides. He had a feeling that his office would be called on to intervene since race relations was what they hired him to do these days.

He seemed to remember a small article about another firebombing in Höchst. The one he was reading now was a bit longer, although it still represented the top command's desire to minimize press coverage of any racially-tinged incidents. If he recalled, the earlier arson attack had been just a couple months ago at an office quonset. He asked his secretary to come into his office. Once she was in the room, he showed her the article he had been reading.

"Do you recall another article about a firebombing in Höchst?"

"I do," answered his secretary. "In the *Stars &*

Stripes."

"Can you find it for me, please?" She left the room. "Look at the library if we don't have that day's paper."

Ana

It was a terrible meeting. Schlecht. The people in the deserter group will not help the man that is named Gene escape to Sweden. I know it is not because he is black because we have helped many blacks leave the army. It is because he is involved with the arson in Höchst. When I brought up the idea of helping him, there was a very large argument. I also mentioned that another man from Höchst wishes to leave. A white man. They asked why. I told them it was because he was accused of setting a fire to the office of an officer who is very racist. Ulf, an older man, held up his hand to shout what do you mean he started a fire? I told the group that there have been many incidents of racial attacks and prejudice by this officer and some of the other officers that work with him. It was causing quite a bit of anger and unhappiness. The white man was friends with the black GIs and was tired of the prejudice. He got angry and tried to burn down the office at night when there was nobody inside. Now he is under suspicion and wants to leave. He never wanted to be in the army but was drafted.

This caused Ulf to repeat his point that we were Pazifisten and did not support violence and could not help those that were suspected of violence. But, I said, we have helped men go to Sweden that have killed people in Vietnam. Ulf and his wife said that was different. Those men, said Olga Ulf's wife, had given up violence as a method to solve things. This young man who I talked about was using violence to try and solve a problem. Then the seven of us had a very long debate about violence. Is it possible to commit violence against a building? Is all violence wrong or is some justified when it does not harm persons but prevents persons from being harmed?

After thirty minutes, there was no resolution. Then Janns, a young man, asked about the other GI I wanted to help leave, the black man. His name is Gene, I said. He is one of the men that has been the subject of the razismus and prejudice. The officers said he tried to burn some military police vehicles because they are used to stop the GIs in Höchst from exercising their rights. He is very afraid right now, I said. He thinks he will end up in a prison in the United States for a long time. He is staying at a besetzende Haus presently but wants to leave. Then again there was a strong argument from Ulf against helping this man. I said to Ulf that I think he is afraid of the Bundeskriminalamt. He said maybe he is. I told him that this bureaucracy is mostly concerned with the Rote Armee Fraktion who are robbing banks. Ulf made the argument that because these men are suspected of fire-bombing that maybe the Polizisten think they are part of the RAF. I had not thought of that. We ended the meeting after that.

I think I will help these GIs to leave. I think maybe Janns will also help. We will see what happens then. I think the people in this group are afraid because of the RAF. They do not want to be thought of the same way so now they will not take risks. I do not agree with the RAF but that is because they are trying to create a revolution when the conditions are not there.

Victor

At least twelve hours. That was how long Victor figured he had been sitting in the small dark room. At first, some German cops had sat with him and talked. He tried not to answer them by pretending he did not understand but they seemed to know he understood German pretty well. They spoke fairly good English. So he had admitted that yes, he knew the Turkish guys he had been busted with in a rooming house near the Hauptbahnhof. Victor was buying some heroin for his own use. The Turks were counting the money they had just been paid and Victor was laying out a line on some foil getting ready to smoke the stuff. This was called chasing the dragon.. He had rolled up a bill and was holding his Zippo under the foil when the room filled up with uniformed Polizisten. He dropped the foil, the bill, and the Zippo but not the rest of the powder. The cops searched his pants and found a little bit of hashish and the smack. Next thing he knew the cuffs were on him and he was in the back of a police car. He figured he was fucked. When they got him to the station he sat in a lit cell for at least an hour while they processed the Turks. Both of them disappeared after that. Victor didn't know whether they were being deported, sent to another jail or if they were working for the cops. He didn't know anything — he was just waiting. Finally, a couple other Polizisten took him from the cell he had been waiting in and brought him into another room. They took his fingerprints, his ID, and asked his address. He didn't tell them about Roter Stern but said he was living in the room where he got busted. His ID was a fake that a friend of Ana's had made for him. The name on it was Viktor Buddenbaum. Age 22 born 1950 January 21. The cop then took him to the room where he still was. They asked him how long he had been buying heroin and if he was addicted. He told them that it was the first time he had ever bought it, which was kind of true because always before he had given the money to someone else that made the actual purchase. Then they asked him if he sold heroin. He said nein and they asked him if he sold other drugs. Victor did not answer. The Polizisten then left the room for a long time. He was almost asleep when they came back in. They seemed to be a bit drunk. He guessed the time was after midnight, perhaps two in the morning. The cops sat in the room talking to each other and ignoring him. He was starting to feel sick; sweaty and nauseous. This was probably because he hadn't done any heroin since early the previous day and his body felt the lack, something that was happening more frequently ever since Victor quit selling hashish at the Zoom Club and started doing more heroin. The amount of hash available had decreased considerably and the amount of heroin had increased. Victor had never really thought about it until now but there was probably some kind of intentional relationship between those two phenomena. He had certainly fallen for it, just moved right off the hash and into the heroin. At the same time, he and Ana seemed to be drifting apart. It wasn't because of anything she had or hadn't done, but because he was bored with being in a relationship. She didn't ask much of him; she even supported him without complaining. Victor was tired of answering any questions about where he had been when he didn't come home for a couple days, assuming she was trying to bust him for his heroin use. The closer truth might be that he was feeling guilty about using. He knew hard drug use was completely verboten at the Roter Stern. The ratty little guy that first got him high had been beaten up and thrown out on the street once it was proven he was bringing the stuff into the commune. Besides the cops, another person Victor did not want to run into was Porgy. He would know right away Victor was using.

His whole body felt like shit. Cold then hot then cold then hot. How did that John and Yoko song go? Cold turkey has got me all wrong? That's how his body felt. It was like his body's thermostat was broken. Sweat then chills and all the time incredible nausea.

Oh well, maybe I can kick in this room. My jones couldn't be that bad could it? It's only been three or four weeks since I started using steadily. Right after that big rally with Angela Davis's sister was over. Before Ana got caught up in the deserter stuff again. I hope I get out of this fuckin' situation. I got tickets to see the Grateful Dead in a couple weeks.

A light came on, waking Victor from a fitful sleep. Three men were in the room besides him: one of the German cops from before, an undercover guy who looked like a hippie and then some guy Victor swore looked like his Drill Instructor in boot camp. The last guy had a very large body, short blonde hair and was ugly as sin. Big old head, mean eyes and bad breath.

"Guten Tag," said the German cop. The hippie-looking guy smiled. Victor remembered him from Zoom Club. That meant Victor was in trouble for dealing even if he never sold to this guy who was always there watching. This cop knew what Victor did for a living. The ugly guy sat down on one of the two chairs the cops had brought in with them.

"Ja. Das ist er," said the hippie-looking narc. He shook the other two men's hands and left the room. The German cop sat in the other available chair. Nobody said anything for about five minutes. Victor was feeling a little better than he had before he fell asleep but he still felt like shit. The ugly guy moved closer. Victor realized how big he was and how muscular. The guy's breath really stunk, like his uncle's farm in the spring when he spread the cowshit on the fields.

"You" said the ugly guy. "We know you are not German. In fact, we have identified you as Victor Willard and you are more than AWOL. You are wanted for assault and desertion." His face was two inches away from Victor and he knew how bad his breath smelled. "Plus whatever the Krauts want you for." Victor said nothing. He was working at trying not to puke. The combination of this guy's breath and his heroin-sickness was causing major turbulence in his stomach. Of course this guy was a cop. Victor wondered whether he was CID, MI or just a plain old MP. Either way, he had a feeling that he was screwed and wondered what they were going to do with him.

The German cop and the American conversed quietly over Victor's fate. They spoke mostly in English. The American probably didn't know enough German to carry on a conversation. It sounded like Victor would be going with the American, which probably meant a court martial and a few years in Leavenworth or some other military prison. Once the conversation ended, the German looked at Victor.

"Wir kommen zurück," he told Victor. They turned off the light and locked the door behind them. It must have been thirty minutes or so when the door reopened. The two cops were back and the German one had a plate with Brotchen and some kind of sliced meat on it. He offered it to Victor who thought he might as well try to eat even though he felt like shit. He didn't think he would be able to, but at the same time knew he should. As they turned to leave, the American told Victor to get some sleep. He turned out the light again, making the room pitch black. Victor tried a piece of the sliced meat. It was no use, his body had no desire to ingest any kind of food. He fell back asleep.

The Ugly American guy was back. He leaned into Victor's face.

"You fuck! Sgt. Haywood was a friend of mine."

"Haywood?" Thought Victor. "Does he mean that asshole sergeant that got McRice sent to the stockade?"

He kept quiet. Haywood was part of the reason Victor was where he was. Fuck him. Victor was glad he got busted for being a racist asshole. Where could these two have been friends? Hell?

"He saved my ass in Vietnam a couple times! When we were chasing down bums like you doing stuff they weren't supposed to be doing instead of fighting Charlie. I've busted hundreds of druggies like you "

"They weren't friends in hell, but close enough," thought Victor. "Vietnam. While everyone else was fighting the gooks he was going after GIs with Haywood. Figures."

Haywood and this guy, who Victor was not looking forward to dealing with, were narco cops. That explained Haywood's hatred of him, McRice and half of the other guys in his former unit, all of them dopers. Victor sat very still even though he felt like lying down on the floor and trying to sleep. He knew he had to keep cool. He listened to the ugly guy yell.

"Yeah. Because of you and that nigger friend of yours, my buddy Haywood lost a stripe and his job here. Now he's pushing paper and telling punks like you to sweep parking lots in Texas. If this Kraut wasn't watching me I'd kick your ass right now." Sweat was beading up on the Ugly American's face. Victor didn't react. So Haywood was back in Texas, probably Fort Hood. He thought it was a good place for a cracker like him. From what he heard the scene outside the base in Killeen was pretty wild. Some friends from his unit came out of there and said there were lots of local chicks and lots of Mexican weed. Victor retched. He never really felt like he was hooked.

The Ugly American leaned into Victor's face and spoke in a low voice. It was probably the closest thing to a whisper the guy could manage. "I don't agree with what I'm going to tell you but I've got orders from people higher up and you are going to listen carefully to what we tell you, you sorry piece of shit." The German uniformed cop came back into the room. He pulled a small glass vial from his coat pocket and held it in front of Victor. He began to talk. The Ugly American took a couple steps back and watched.

"Mein Freund," began the German cop. "I am

with a special group of policemen from many countries--Germany, England, Italia, United States, Greece, Turkei--that is working to prevent the heroin from coming into my country. We are asking you to help. It depends on how much you can do and how much you know..."

Victor wasn't sure what was going on. Was this cop asking him to narc? That wasn't going to happen, Victor thought. Not only could he get his ass killed but he had some moral qualms about it. The German cop continued.

"You are how do you say?" He looked at the Ugly American. "Small fry?" The Ugly American nodded. "Ja. Small fry. But you know many people for such a small fry. We know you live in der Roter Stern. We know you sell hashish in the Zoom Club. We know you buy hashish from a Turkish citizen. Und we know more about you also."

"Yeah," piped in the Ugly American. "We know you got hooked recently and we know you hang out with some political folks we are interested in."

"I do not care about the politics," said the German cop. "That is for you Americans. But my friend Mr. Crooks here," he nodded toward the Ugly American. "Say that we can kill two birds with one stone, Ja?" He smiled and set the tube of powder on the small table near Victor.

"How do you feel?" asked the German cop. "You have a look like you are very sick."

Victor said nothing. He couldn't really talk and was trying not to dry heave. All he could smell was the vomit from when he had thrown up earlier which made him even more nauseous. Crooks stepped forward and leaned in to Victor's face. He breathed his foul breath.

"What can you tell us about that commune you live in?" asked Crooks. "Who lives there? Are there Baader-Meinhof people there?"

Victor looked up from his misery. Baader-Meinhof? He must mean the RAF. Victor knew that the politicos at the Red Star debated about the RAF a lot but it seemed to him that most people didn't agree with their underground struggle thing. He wasn't really sure since he really didn't pay attention to the politics, especially since he had gotten into heroin.

"Why do you wanna' know?" asked Victor. The German cop unscrewed the cap of the vial and tapped a very small amount of the powder on the table. The pile was maybe as big as a match head.

"You can sniff this now," he said. "If you do what we tell you to do."

Victor wished he had more willpower but when all was said and done he had very little. He leaned forward and snorted the powder. It hit the back of his head in milliseconds. Within three minutes he felt as if he had never been sick. Within five minutes he felt like he was floating and in ten minutes he was nodding. The German cop gave the vial to Crooks and

left the room. Crooks remained. He had some instructions to go over with Victor when he came to.

Martha

Dad just doesn't get it, thought Martha. Porgy is a really cool, smart cat. If he would just give him a chance. She was surprised at how pissed off the Colonel was. Fortunately, he backed off from forbidding her to see Porgy at all once she agreed not to skip school anymore. He knew she considered education as important as he did.

Porgy and Martha left the apartment. Porgy said he would take Martha to the Strassenbahn and wait with her until it came. The only other person waiting at the stop was a man with a beard and a turban. Porgy guessed he was a Sikh. Martha asked him how he knew.

"When I was a kid my dad was stationed in Pakistan. He was one of the few Army guys on an Air Force station. The base was a small place in this town called Peshawar. Besides a couple GIs, we was the only blacks on base. Most of the kids was cool but some of the parents were total crackers. I wasn't allowed in some people's homes and shit. My parents would give parties and some people wouldn't show up because we were black."

"Wow," said Martha. "That's not your usual assignment."

"In retrospect, I'm glad my dad got sent there. Before that we was always on military bases in the States and it seemed like we got the worst houses especially when my dad was in Louisiana. Crackers everywhere, if you know what I mean. I don't know if you remember since you're a few years younger but the Army used to be as racist as the fuckin' Klan especially when you were in the South. It's not as bad now even though it's still pretty bad."

"They need the brothers to do the killing for them, so they improve their race relations," said Martha. "Plus with them dying means fewer white guys die."

"I don't know if it's that simple but you're probably right. Anyhow, when we got to Pakistan, it was the very early sixties and the assignment was pretty damned exotic. It was weird, even the NCOs had servants if they wanted them. We had a guy who did our gardening but my mom didn't want anybody else in the house so unlike my friends we didn't have a bearer." Porgy smiled, remembering the tricks he and his friends used to play on the gardener while he slept in the afternoon. Silly shit like stealing his cigarettes and putting them between his toes or hiding his hubble-bubble--his water pipe. The guy, whose name was Esau, was very good natured. He called the white guys little Sahibs and Porgy little brother.

"How did you all entertain yourselves?" asked Martha.

"There was a swimming pool and a bowling alley on base. Unlike the South, the blacks and the whites all used the same pool. Plus a golf course and they used the chapel as a movie theater. Every Saturday afternoon they showed serials and a feature for us kids. It was pretty Americanized on base," remembered Porgy. "My parents always took me and my brother shopping in downtown Peshawar when they went. I always acted like I hated it, but really it was pretty cool just 'cause it was so different. Open air market. Guys walking around with swords and turbans. No Pakistani women at all because of the Muslim thing."

"How come you didn't want to go?"

"It wasn't cool to think the Pakistanis were cool," answered Porgy. "Typical shit just like a lot of Americans here call the Germans Krauts. They act like colonialist motherfuckers because they afraid. My dad asked me while he was dying if I knew why he and Mom insisted we go on them jaunts. I told him no, and his answer was that he wanted us to know that not everyone in the world was white. Living on military bases and in the US made us colored people wonder sometimes, and I quote him, if we really was few and far between, when in reality we're the majority in the world."

"Sounds like something Malcolm X would say,"

noted Martha.

"Yeah, that's what I said when he told me," laughed Porgy. The Strassenbahn was approaching. Martha wrapped herself around Porgy and kissed him.

"See ya'," she got on the streetcar. Porgy headed in another direction.

Ana

Ana was on the Number 3 Strassenbahn. She wondered where Victor was. It had been a couple days since he had been around. They hadn't really argued but she did mention it seemed he was drifting apart from her. He didn't answer. He kissed her and they started to make love but he did not get an erection. That was okay with her but it seemed to bother him. She wondered if she didn't excite him anymore or if he was doing too many drugs. Now she was on her way to meet the two GIs that had committed the fire-bombings in Höchst. Porgy had set up the meeting but did not want to be there. In fact, Porgy had remarked that he needed to keep some distance because he thought he was being watched. Maybe it was because of his young girlfriend, he said. She planned to meet the two men at a Gasthaus in Rödelheim, not too far from where she had grown up. It was a new establishment that had a disco on Friday nights that was popular with black GIs. The number 3 Strassenbahn stopped very near it. She got off and walked a block and a half. After finding a table near the back of the Gasthaus, she went to use the bathroom. The place was almost empty. That was good. When she returned to her table, the proprietor came over and introduced himself. He was probably about thirty years old and had longish hair. Ana ordered a glass of Henninger beer and some pommes frites. She told the man she was expecting some friends from America that were visiting her family. While she was still drinking her first beer, both men showed up and found her. They introduced themselves, ordered beers and a plate of smoked pork and Rotkraut each. After another beer, the white guy, whose name was Ray, spoke.

"Ana, me and Gene here are wondering how the hell we are gonna' get out of town. I can't speak for Gene but I am nervous as hell. Even though the place I'm staying seems cool I just can't shake my paranoia."

"Hey brother." Gene sounded relaxed. "Give the lady a chance to explain some stuff. All right?"

Ray sat back. Ana ordered three more Henningers. After they arrived and the proprietor went back to watching a soccer game on a television behind the bar, she explained the process.

"What we do is this." She began. "First we need passport photos of you. Then we find a name that we can use for each of you. I have contacts that will make passports with visa stamps and everything you need. They are how do you say flawless. The gangsters use them all of the time. It will not cost you because you have no money and I have funds I will take from. Then we must come up with a story in case you are stopped on the way there. I think it is best for you to take a train because the Zollarbeiter--the customs workers--do not check people's passports as closely on a train as they do for those traveling by auto. I will contact people in Sweden who will meet you and they will help you find a place to live and maybe work. You must not do any drugs or have anything illegal with you because you are illegal enough. You must also practice your new name and personal information because that will be who you are once it is designed. I think we can have you ready to go in ten days. How does that sound?"

Gene nodded okay. Ray said nothing. "I don't know, man. It seems too long."

"I am sorry," said Ana. "That is best we can do." She had dealt with men like Ray before. She was usually able to calm them down so they did not blow their cover. She looked at Gene. "Are you okay traveling together?"

"I guess."

"We will have you on the same train but not as traveling companions. Perhaps you can pretend to meet up on the train and then stay together?"

"That might work," agreed Gene.

"How are the places you are staying?" asked Ana. Gene said his was fine. Ray said he slept most of the time. They finished up their meals, had a couple more beers and then walked together to the Strassenbahn stop. Ana told them she would see them in a week with the paperwork and then all she would need to do was get the photos from them. After that they should be ready to go. She told Ray she would try to move the departure date up. He looked more relaxed.

After making sure the two men got on the streetcar, Ana went back to the Gasthaus and drank another beer. Then she wandered around Rödelheim. It had been a while since she had been there. With the exception of a couple more small factories and some different names on certain storefronts, it was pretty much the same as she remembered it growing up. The river that ran through the town still smelled like sewage in some areas, and was beautiful in others. The Konditorei where she bought Brotchen every day was still there, as was the Metzgerei. The little Bahnhof looked exactly the same. Simpler times, she thought to herself, all gone. She caught a streetcar back into Frankfurt around 10 in the evening. She hoped Victor would be at the commune.

Victor

Victor came to. The ugly American named Crooks was still there. He wondered how long he had been nodding. The dream he had while nodded out on the heroin had been about Gudrun Enslinn of the Baader-Meinhof/ RAF. She was a good looking blonde. If they wanted to recruit teenagers to their group she could be their best poster girl. After rubbing his eyes and asking for a drink which Crooks provided, Victor sat up straight. Crooks began to talk.

"Look here, punk. I still don't agree with the Krauts here but it's there business. My role is to ask you about some political shit you probably know about. Let's start with that Angela Davis. I know you were at the rally. We have pictures of you in the back. We also know you live at the Red Star place across from the PX. Is that cute little German girl your girl-friend? We have pictures of the two of you together. You know you're not the first hippie she's fucked, don't you? We know she's involved in a lot of com-mie shit around the university and with niggers. What can you tell me about that? Also, there were some firebombings out in Höchst recently and the assholes responsible for them have disappeared. We have no fucking idea where they are. Maybe you can help us on that? We need to know if they are part of the Baader-Meinhof group. Those are just a few of the questions we want answered and you are going to help us answer them. You can't back out now. If you do it will be a guaranteed three years in German prison and then ten or so more in Leavenworth. That's in Kansas if you didn't know. It is not a fun place. You got yourself into a big fucking situation and the only way you will ever get out of it is by helping us. That's the deal. The Krauts will keep you supplied with your heroin and will probably even give you enough to try and set up some big boys in the business. I will give you money but I want answers to some questions starting with the ones I just asked. Do I need to write them down to make myself very clear?"

Victor shook his head no. He knew he was fucked and had to figure something out. But he wanted the heroin and he didn't want to go to jail. It made him feel so much better once he had that snort. Being that sick was not worth repeating. This guy didn't seem all that smart to Victor. Maybe he could give him something without giving him anything. It was worth a try.

"Good. We understand each other." He brought his ugly face and nasty breath close to Victor's face. "I want bodies, you understand. Bodies! You can start by getting me those firebombers." Crooks gave Victor seventy-five DM and left the room. The German cop came back in. He handed Victor the vial of powder and told him to be careful because it was very strong. After telling Victor he wanted an arrest of someone higher in the drug traffic chain by the end of the month, preferably a Turkish citizen, Victor was given some new clothes and told to shower, dress and leave.

Martha

Martha felt good. She and Porgy were more than compatible. The sex was great and the conversation was equally good. If it meant she could hang with him for a few more months, she would consider starting college late. She wasn't sure, but thought he said he was out in September. She wondered if Yale would wait. Her father probably wouldn't, though. The streetcar arrived downtown.

It was a beautiful day in the plaza at the Hauptwache, sunny and warm. People were taking their time doing their Saturday errands instead of rushing around like they would if it were cold. There was some kind of street theater taking place diagonally across from where Martha sat. It seemed to be about the housing crisis in Frankfurt. From what Martha understood of the situation, a few speculators had bought apartment buildings through some kind of sweetheart deal with the banks and the postwar power structure and now they were trying to sell them to other rich folks who wanted to turn them into much more lucrative office buildings. Meanwhile the cost of housing was creeping

up and making it unaffordable to students, Gastarbeiter and many other working people. Or maybe it was
the first group of speculators that wanted to turn the
houses into offices. Either way a bunch of buildings
had been taken over by students and Gastarbeiter who
were now living in them. These folks had been joined
by more respectable types that lived in the same neighborhoods and did not want office buildings as neigh-
bors. The theater piece was making the adhoc group of
spectators laugh.

She looked at her watch and saw it was time to
transfer to the U-Bahn and meet her mom at the PX.
Martha walked the distance to the Hauptwache U-
Bahn and went down the escalator. She thought she
saw that guy Victor across the way near the bath-
rooms. If it was him, he wasn't looking too good. It
seemed that he was a lot skinnier than she remembered and his hair looked real stringy. She looked
again but he was gone. Making a mental note to ask
Porgy about him, she continued to the train.

There were a few German hippies smoking hash
near the escalator where an entrance to the service
area was. The whole area smelled like the drug. The
more conservative shoppers were hurrying past muttering disgust and looking away. Little kids asked
their parents what the smell was and other students
and adolescents walked by with a knowing smile. A
pair of Polizei walked towards the group of hippies.
The group scattered and the police walked on, their

presence having been responded to. The shopping continued as before. Martha heard a train coming and ran
down the rest of the stairs. She got on just before the
doors closed.

Porgy/Ana

Porgy was supposed to meet Ana after her meetup with Gene and Ray. He had been keeping his distance from the two arsonists but was willing to help in whatever way he could that didn't draw attention. Ana had promised to let him know how her meeting with the two men had gone. Ray seemed incredibly nervous the last time Porgy had seen him, which didn't bode well and made the other cat Gene want to go it alone. Ana felt it would be better if the two left together with Gene acting as a calming influence on Ray. Once they got to Sweden, he could do his own thing. If the plan Ana was working on went well, the two men would be gone in two weeks. Porgy had to admit the whole thing stressed him out a bit. He didn't want to get busted for something as stupid as trying to burn up some military vehicles but he under-stood the need to support these guys and get them out of Germany. He was near the spot in the park where he was supposed to meet Ana, who was standing un-der a tree waiting. She waved hello. After exchanging greetings, she gave Porgy the update. Once she was done, he thanked her and turned around to leave.

"Porgy," Ana sounded a little upset. Porgy turned back around. "Have you seen Victor?"

"No. Not in a couple weeks. Why?" Porgy wondered what was up. "Haven't you seen him?"

"I have not seen him very much in these past three weeks." She looked at Porgy. "I think he is what do you say drifting? From me."

"Why would he do that?" asked Porgy. He wasn't so certain that this might not be a good thing, but he hated to see Ana so distraught.

"I do not know. We were making much love and getting along, ich habe gedacht." Ana truly had no idea what was wrong. She hoped Porgy might know something.

"Does he come to the commune?" asked Porgy.

"Only when he is tired or sick," answered Ana. "I do not ask him where he goes but I wonder. I am afraid he is in trouble. I am lately wishing I did not love him so much, but I do. Do you know what I mean? If I did not love him like this, I would not worry about him."

"Yeah, Ana, I understand. Love will make you crazy sometimes. Let me know if you don't see him tonight or tomorrow," said Porgy. "I'll look for him. When you do see him you should talk with him about your concerns. No man should do that to you."

"Danke." She kissed him and headed back to Roter Stern.

Victor

Victor couldn't believe his luck. From the worst luck ever getting busted to walking around with at least a gram of incredible heroin in his pocket, given to him by the cops. After leaving the police station he had gone straight to Tarachi's apartment. Tarachi was not in Turkey like Victor expected and invited him in. They ate and drank for a while then Tarachi brought out some hashish. After smoking and listening to Pink Floyd, they fell asleep. The next day Tarachi asked Victor if he could get some acid to take back to his country. Victor was unsure because there had been a shortage of the stuff, but said yes . The Grateful Dead were coming, so who knew what their entourage would be carrying. Tarachi continued, asking about the hash scene. Victor told him about the busts and subsequent shortage. Victor ducked into the bathroom and took a small snort of the heroin. When he didn't come out after five minutes Tarachi went in to see what was the matter. Victor was on the floor. Tarachi stood him up and threw water in his face.

"What the hell?" yelled Victor, coming to. He saw

Tarachi holding the smack. "That is some incredible dope"

Tarachi shook his head. "I can see that. I thought you were dead, asshole. My brother likes heroin. He is addicted to this. You cannot take it pure. You must dilute it. Or you will die. "

Victor looked at Tarachi. "Do you want some?"

Tarachi shook his head no. "I do not want to do anthing that addicting, but we can make money if you can get more. Can you get more?"

"I think so," answered Victor.

Tarachi looked straight at Victor. "I will tell my brother to come. He can help us make this a good strength. He knows people that will buy. International businessmen. "

Victor sat down on a couch in Tarachi's living room. This was almost too easy. The two men made plans to meet in two days at a club Tarachi's brother belonged to near Rhein Main Flughafen, Tarachi told Victor to wear a nice looking jacket.

Ana

It was an incredibly warm afternoon for Frankfurt in March, probably close to 25° Celsius. Ana and Victor had spent most of the past twenty hours in bed. He came back to the commune not long after Ana's meeting with Porgy. She knew she should be mad but she was so damn happy to see him that they were making love within ten minutes of his arrival. They smoked some hashish he had and then they had more sex. Victor was not sick and he seemed happy. She hoped it would last. Not wanting to pry she had yet to ask him where he had been. Victor, for his own reasons, had not made much conversation either. It seemed that the both of them preferred conversing through their bodies.

They were still in bed, naked and leaning against the wall, their arms around each other. Victor had opened the window in the room they used and there was a warm breeze. It smelled like spring. Ana lay her head on Victor's shoulder.

"It is good to have you here." She said. She ran her hand across his chest, stopping to play with a small tuft of hair on his chest. "I thought you were too angry with me and would not come back.”

Victor adjusted his position. “I was not mad at you. I just needed to have some time.” This wasn't a complete lie. The last time they had been together Ana and he had had words over his appearance. He had been pretty out of it. “How have you been?”

“I have been okay except for wondering about you,” replied Ana. “I was afraid you were dead or in the jail.” Victor took a breath.

“I was staying with some friends in Oberursel.” He lied. “Then I stayed with Tarachi. That's where I got that hashish.”

“It's good Scheiss.” Said Ana. “Let's smoke some more.” She began to kiss his chest and moved her face downwards. Victor found the pipe and lit up the remaining piece. Ana licked his navel. They smoked some more, made love and fell asleep. When they awoke it was dark.

Victor was sitting on the side of the mattress. “Do you still want to go to the Grateful Dead concert?”

Ana nodded. “Ja. I have been listening to that album you gave me. Anthem of the Sun. I like the music but the lyrics seem... obscure?”

“I don't know a lot about them, but I can tell you that that song that goes “Spanish Lady came to me she laid on me this rose...?”

“Ja?”

“Well, you have heard of Ken Kesey and the Electric Koolaid Acid Test?” Asked Victor.

Ana nodded. "Yes. I have not read the book but my friends have."

"That song is about the bus and the LSD trips and the events they called the Acid tests." explained Victor. "The Grateful Dead were a big part of that experience."

Ana smiled. "You know more than I do."

"There's this guy named Peter I used to know before I went AWOL. He goes to the high school here. He is into the Grateful Dead . What I know about them I learned from him."

Victor climbed back under the sheets. He was hungry but did not want to leave the good feeling he had. After meeting up with Tarachi's brother, who had taken them to his hotel room and shown Victor the right proportion of cut to apply to the heroin, Victor was able to control how high he got on the stuff. While he was with Ana he had been taking just enough to prevent sickness. That way he could still fuck. So far everything was working.

"So," asked Victor. "What have you been doing?"

Ana shrugged her shoulders. "There have been meetings for the Angela Davis conference in June. There have also been meetings about police and the besetzende Häuser. I have been going to those and I have been working here some. It was a while since I did my part to keep the collective going so now I am making up for that."

Victor nodded. He had decided not tell her about his arrest, especially since it had turned out the way it did. Things were going too smoothly to bring that up.

"Oh ja," continued Ana. "I am helping two GIs leave the country."

"Two?" asked Victor. "At the same time? Isn't that unusual?"

Ana nodded. "Yes. But they must leave quickly. Have you heard of the firebombings in Höchst?"

Victor shook his head no, even though he guessed these bombings were the ones referred to by Crooks.

"There have been some racial incidents between the officers and the black GIs in Höchst. Someone has thrown a firebomb into an officer's office and then someone else has tried to burn up the motor pool. These two men are the ones who are suspected of doing this and they need to leave. I think in one week." Ana was trying to be vague. Although she didn't tell Victor the details of the attacks as she knew them or the fact that she was working on this desertion mostly by herself, she did feel as if she could tell him the minimal facts. What was he going to do with the information anyhow?

"Wow." Was all Victor said in reply.

Ana gave Victor a kiss and stood up. It was time to get something to eat. She was woozy from all the sex and hash. Too bad we can't live on that alone, she thought. She headed to the kitchen area and Victor stayed in bed.

He thought about his meeting with Crooks scheduled for the day after tomorrow. There was no way he was going to let him get his hands on Ana. How could he pull off giving the guy information that wouldn't hurt Ana and even better wouldn't give him anything? There had to be some way that he could tell the asshole about the deserters but make it so they got to Sweden before the CID or Military Intelligence could do anything about it. He wasn't looking forward to the meeting at all.

Ana was back with some juice, bread and cheese. Victor was playing guitar. She took off her robe and climbed back under the sheet with the food. He just couldn't do her wrong. Getting out of the mess he was in was not going to be easy.

Victor

Tarachi's brother was something else. He really was a high-powered businessman. The club we had lunch at was some kind of place that international businessmen and jet setters hung out at while they're waiting for a plane in Frankfurt. The lunch was incredible and as far as I could tell Dean -- that's Tarachi's brother's name -- didn't pay for it. It's probably part of some kind of exorbitant club fees. The liquor was flowing and the food just kept coming. Dean's English was perfect. No accent or nothing and full of what Uncle Jack called fifty cent words. After a leisurely lunch he took us to his hotel room at the airport hotel and we sat around smoking hashish. Then he asked to see the heroin and he was impressed. He cut it up with some kind of lactose or some powder so that I could sniff it without passing out. He showed me exactly how much to take and said if people were going to buy it to inject--his word--then it should be cut even more. I gave him half of the vial and left. He told me he would get in touch with me through Tarachi who would then introduce me to some of "his men" if he was interested. I figure I'll let that German cop know I found someone who wants to cop. I hope Dean's "men" are Turkish since that German cop wanted to bust Turks. Who knows why, other than Turks are like Germany's black people, or maybe more like Puerto Ricans and Mexicans. The Germans only want their cheap labor and otherwise they shit on them every chance they get.

On my way to that meeting with the cops right now. It's out of town up past Oberursel at some house. After I get off the Strassenbahn, I have to catch a cab and take it to the house. I think I can keep the German cop off my back and even get some more of that smack as long as he likes my story. Crooks is going to be harder mostly because he's stupider and it's a political bust that he wants to make. Fucking fascist. I ain't giving up any info on Ana though. I figure I can put him off with some story about something and then tell him I need a number to call him if something comes up. Then after I know those cats going to Sweden are good and gone I can call him and act like they are still in Germany. That way I give them a lead but it won't do them no good. I wish I could tell Ana what's up but it would just confuse shit and I don't know what telling her would do anyhow.

Here's Oberursel. Looks like there's a cab I can take already at the station. Good, I didn't want to wait.

Victor got in the cab and gave the driver the address. During the ride up into the Taunus he recalled his trip up in the mountains with Ana. It was so recent yet so long ago. They arrived at the house in an hour. The driver stopped, turned around and told Victor the fare was twenty DM. He paid and got out. The German cop who had provided the vial of heroin was looking out the window, out of uniform. Victor went in, removed his jacket and found a chair. The German cop asked him how he had done. Victor told him he found a person interested in buying a fair amount of the heroin. After explaining it was a Turkish businessman, the German cop smiled, gave Victor some more heroin and two hundred DM. They set up another meeting to discuss details. Then Crooks came into the room. Victor didn't look up. This guy made him nervous.

"Hey, Mr. Willard," Crooks sat his big frame down in a seat across from Victor. He smiled an ugly grin and looked into Victor's face. "You look better than the last time I saw you."

"Thanks," said Victor. This guy was still just as ugly, Victor thought.

"What do you have for me?" asked Crooks. "Any information on those commie friends of yours?"

"No." Victor stood up and began to pace.

"Sit down," said Crooks. "Are you hungry? Oh I forgot junkies don't eat."

Victor sat back down. He tried to keep quiet, afraid he might say something he would regret.

"Have you heard anything about firebombings?" Crooks moved his chair closer to Victor.

Victor shook his head no. He wasn't going to let on that he knew a thing.

"Don't you read the papers? The *Stars and Stripes* or the *Overseas Weekly*?"

"Not very often," answered Victor. "Not since I left the base."

"Well," began Crooks. "There were a couple of Molotov cocktails thrown at military facilities in Höchst a few weeks ago. We suspect that the acts were done by GIs, but we think there may be a connection to the Baader Meinhof people. Either way, we want to find the people that did this before it becomes a trend. You might remember those two niggers the commies were calling the Ramstein Two? We threw the book at them for the same reason. Shit, we had to get them off the street."

The Pentagon was worried about race relations in Germany, afraid it could get as bad as it was in Vietnam. The Colonel's race relations office was involved in the firebombing case because the fellows suspected of it were black and most of the officers in were white. Crooks had orders to find the arsonists.

Victor shifted uncomfortably. He wondered if this asshole knew that a couple guys were AWOL from that unit in Höchst and were trying to desert. He hoped not.

As if reading Victor's mind, his interrogator continued, "There's two punks that have been AWOL from that unit since the last incident. One white kid and one nigger. We don't know where they are. You find them and deliver them to me for questioning and I'll leave you alone for a few weeks. Maybe even give you a chance to slip out of the country if you know what I mean."

He knew. Victor weighed his words carefully. "I might be able to help you." He spoke slowly. "Do you have a number I can reach you at?"

"What do you know?" Crooks yelled, hoping to get Victor to reveal more than he wanted to. "You can't play me, asshole."

Watch me, thought Victor.

"I know these two guys that are staying here and there. They are talking about leaving once they get some paperwork together. I just heard about it at a bar I hang out in."

"The name of the bar?"

"Sexy Sexy Sexy. It's--" began Victor.

"I know where it is! Made a few busts there a year ago." Crooks reached into his pocket. He handed Victor a piece of paper with a phone number on it. "Memorize this number and the one that Kraut gave you and then get rid of those papers. Call me in two days and let me know any new information. If you don't, I will send some MPs to talk with you in some place very public and make sure they let whoever is watching know that you are working for the police. Do you understand?"

Victor nodded his head yes and left the room. The German cop had called a cab and instructed Victor to get in and ride it into Frankfurt. Victor did as he was instructed. Crooks laughed at how easy it was to intimidate Willard and, for that matter, most people he interrogated. His tactics had caused a couple complaints to be registered with his superiors after he brutalized a mouthy suspect with political connections; his uncle was a congressman. His boss told him to modify his interrogation techniques, but he saw no reason to do so. As far as he was concerned, they were fine.

Porgy

I ran into Victor today. Hadn't seen the cat in a few weeks. That boy is some fucked. His eyes were like pinheads. All small. I'm guessing he's doing heroin. We talked for a bit under a tree in the park. I was waiting for Martha and who knows what he was doing. I asked him how he was getting along with Ana and he said okay. They was on the outs for a little bit he said, but things were good again. Then he asked me if I knew anything about the incidents in Höchst. I said only that I read about them in the paper. He said he thought Ana was involved somehow. I said the only way that might be possible was if she was helping the cats responsible to get out of the country. He said yeah, that would make sense. When he got up to leave I told him to not be a fool. He looked at me funny then walked away. I was referring to Ana and being good to her, but I got no ideas what he might have thought I was talking about. I'm guessin' he don't know nothing about me and her.

Porgy was riding the Army bus out to Höchst to

deliver some mail for his boss. The bus, a school bus painted Army green, was half-full. Most of the passengers were housewives returning from the commissary near the main PX in Frankfurt. There was a GI driving, an older black man. His 8-track was playing some Curtis Mayfield soul from his time with the Impressions. Porgy recognized the track playing. "This Is My Country". A white guy was standing up at the front talking with the driver. Both were laughing. Porgy had spent the night before with Martha. Her dad was back in DC and her mom did not seem to mind the two of them being together like her father did. In fact, she had suggested the three have dinner while her husband was gone.

Martha

Martha smiled. She tried to picture Porgy as a kid. Besides being cute as the dickens, he was probably the definition of earnest. It was easy to see him trying to please his mom and his teachers. Being smart and black probably confused some of them, but if he had any young liberal teachers they would have loved him. She wondered if there was such a thing then. Even though she was only five or so years younger than Porgy, she knew the world had changed a lot in that short time, especially when it came to young people's attitudes about race in the US. It was odd to Martha how blacks not even a decade older than her often had a fearful or even subservient role they played around whites. It angered her sometimes but mostly it was just strange. She tried to picture how it must feel to be afraid of people just because they had a different color skin.

Porgy was still earnest. It was one of the attributes that kept Martha interested and that she found endearing. He really did seem to act out of love for the oppressed in his politics. Hell, that's how he acted in his personal life, too, seeing the good in everyone. That was more than Martha could say about most people, including herself. Even her parents, whom she loved, had their moments of hate. As for the other reasons she loved Porgy, Martha smiled to herself, remembering the previous night's passion.

Martha wouldn't say it aloud, but she was glad her father was away. If not for his absence, Porgy would not be coming over. A bit ironically, Louisa had reminded her the night before how much she used to miss her father during his trips away when she was young.

The smells from the kitchen were making her hungry. The menu included pork roast, potatoes and green beans. Porgy was supposed to arrive around 6:30. He had promised to bring some wine and had even asked what kind her mother liked. The doorbell rang and Martha let Porgy in. After a quick kiss, the two went into the kitchen to make introductions.

"Mom," began Martha. "This is Porgy Johnson. Porgy, my mom, Louisa."

Porgy shook the Colonel's wife's hand after setting the bottle of wine on the counter. "It's great to meet you, ma'am."

Louisa smiled. "Make yourself at home, young man." She gestured to the living room. "I'll be with you two in a minute. I have a couple things I need to finish up in here."

Martha led Porgy into the living room and sat in

the nearest sofa. Porgy had never been in the quarters in this particular housing area. He had to admit that, except for certain general's houses, this one was probably the most luxurious he had ever seen on a military base, especially in Frankfurt. There were five rooms on the first floor, including the kitchen, a bedroom and what looked like a bar. There was also a bathroom. The furnishings were heavy dark wood, which seemed to be the case in almost every officer's quarters Porgy had been to during his duties in Frankfurt. The walls had several nice paintings on them, which Porgy assumed belonged to the Colonel and his wife. Louisa came into the living room with three glasses of wine and the bottle of wine.

"Since this is a special occasion, Porgy can do the honors." She handed Porgy the bottle and a corkscrew.

Louisa sat in an armchair opposite the couple. Porgy poured her glass first, then Martha's. He returned to his seat.

"To happiness." Louisa raised her glass. They drank.

"So, Porgy, " began Louisa. "I have to ask. Where did the name Porgy come from? You don't have to tell me..."

"Oh no, it's okay. I have a great-uncle from Georgia whose name is Porgy. Where he got the name nobody knows since his parents died in a fire when he was barely six months old."

"I'm sorry." Louisa sipped on her wine.

"That's okay." Porgy reached for the bottle. He

was drinking faster than he wanted to but attributed it to nervousness. "You didn't know. Anybody else want a little more?" He motioned with the bottle. Louisa held out her glass.

"Martha tells me you grew up in the service?"

"Yes, ma'am." Porgy deferred. "My dad was in for twenty years. He joined not long after it was desegregated."

"Lawrence, my husband, joined a few years after that." Louisa reminisced. "I met him in college in Georgia. After he graduated he joined the Army, went to Korea, got into Officer Candidate School and decided it was what he wanted to do. The first place we were stationed was in Fort Meade, Maryland."

"Dad was in the Air Force at first." Porgy explained. I think he figured there would be less prejudice there. I don't know if that's the case. Either way, he switched to the Army after his Air Force enlistment was up. Still we was always being stationed on Air Force bases."

"I think you're right about the Air Force and prejudice, at least back then," Louisa replied. "Now, I think it's about the same everywhere."

"The Navy still won't give non-whites certain jobs." Martha interjected.

"You're right, Martha." Her mom smiled. Her daughter certainly was vigilant on such matters. "I think dinner's ready. Martha, can you help me carry the food to the table?"

The two women went into the kitchen. Porgy picked up the bottle of wine, his glass and went into the living room. He waited for instructions about where he would be sitting.

Karl

A car was parked outside of the Roter Stern. The make was an older Opel Kadett and relatively invisible. If anyone living in the commune had a car, this model would be one of the most likely they would own. The undercover cops--one German and one American--had been watching Victor's comings and goings for several days. They were hoping to see him with either a Turkish dope dealer or one of the GIs the CID was looking for in regards to the Höchst firebombings. So far they had seen nothing related to either case. Victor Willard came and went at no predictable hours. Sometimes he was accompanied by his girlfriend, whom the German cop was quite familiar with due to her political activities and some heavy involvement with the Frankfurt LSD scene when she was younger, before she had discovered leftist politics. The German cop, named Karl, was the same long-haired narc Victor had seen at the police station. Karl considered the return of Ana Becker into his circle of surveillance to be an opportunity to resolve the tangle of emotions she had once brought to his life. These emotions, foremost of which was anger, had simmered ever since she turned his work on a 1970 LSD arrest into an embarrassing failure. As part of his surveillance, Karl had gone into the files of the Bundeskriminalamt. There he found some files that disclosed which groups she worked with. One of them was a pacifist organization that helped GIs desert. Pacifism wasn't her usual approach, thought Karl to himself.

It was hard to believe it was only a year ago. The protest began like so many others. Ten thousand people mostly students and worker type communists gathering on the Opernplatz. Speakers yelling about the Amerikanisch imperialisten; red and black flags swirling about mixing it up with hundreds of signs, some hand lettered and some professionally printed. The slogans were as typical as the content of the speeches. Amis out of Vietnam. Victory to the Vietnamese people Standard stuff. After gathering in the sunny weather for at least three hours the crowd finally started to move. Out of the Opernplatz towards the Hauptwache then a bit of a reversal and on to the American PX complex for another rally. Karl remembered being given a uniform that morning just for the protest. He and his partner were stationed outside the PX and were told take photos. The cameras they were given were brand new, with automatic shutters. One click and thirteen photos were taken in seven seconds. Like an automatic weapon. He remembered hearing the crowd coming from a kilometer away. The police took their positions, truncheons at the ready, dogs at the sides of their handlers. When the front of the protest reached the intersection in front of the PX they began sitting down in the street. The police with the dogs waded in, pulling individuals from the crowd, taking them behind the police lines and beating them.

Karl and the other policemen with cameras clicked away, their telephoto lenses zooming in and out. It might have been maybe twenty minutes and the intersection was full of protesters sitting down and cops taking them away. Then a more militant element came into the intersection. That group did not sit. They began throwing bricks and other objects at the lines of police slowly surrounding the protesters sitting in the street from three sides. Karl adjusted his lens to focus in the brick throwers who were probably fifty meters from where he stood. His partner did the same. Then everything descended into chaos. More bricks and debris raining on them. Protesters charging police lines and making headway, some of them swinging sticks. Police wildly swinging their nightsticks. Karl never saw his partner turning around to look behind him. Even though the projectiles were landing closer and closer to where he stood, his focus was on the view he saw through his lens. When he did look up from the camera, he saw his partner down on the pavement. His face was not visi-

ble and he wasn't moving. Karl stopped taking pictures, leaned down and turned his partner over. Karl knew instantly that something was seriously wrong. He let go of his camera and summoned a police medic. The medic and his assistants appeared within seconds, stabilized his partner and took him away. He never walked again. That night and the next day Karl pestered the darkroom in the police lab to develop every picture. He was determined to find the person who paralyzed his partner. After three long days of careful study he believed he had found her.

It was Ana Becker, a person all too familiar to Karl. He had slept with her, been in love with her, given her secret police information. She had used him. Her feminine guile and cheap morals had caused him to give her the timing of a drug raid he had worked months on. Never again would he trust a female. Nor would he stop his pursuit of Becker until he knew she was out of circulation. If he couldn't have her, no one would. He presented the evidence to the investigative team looking into the riot. They ignored him. How could he be so certain it was Becker who injured his partner? There were dozens of people in the photos who were throwing things at the police Ana never knew she was the object of such speculation.

While they sat, the topic of Crooks came up. Both men found him a bit comical, mostly because of the way he looked. They weren't alone. When they were together, the Polizisten he teamed with often pantomimed his crew cut, tough guy style, and sweaty underarms. None of them knew whether he was married or what else he did besides work. If anyone had asked him, they would probably have been met with silence. The truth was he was divorced. His ex, a Georgia blonde, waited through three and a half years of him working in Vietnam. He never felt like he deserved her. She didn't cheat, didn't get fat, and didn't turn into an alcoholic. When Crooks finally came stateside after those three plus years chasing down wayward GIs in the war zone he accused her of infidelity. No matter what she said or did she could not convince him otherwise. Even though he was at most a moderate drinker in Vietnam, his unfounded suspicions burned a fire of jealousy so hot the only thing that would cool it was more and more alcohol. Although he never hit her, his verbal assaults killed the love she had tended so carefully during his absence. Her parents introduced their daughter to an attorney friend of theirs. They wanted her to file for divorce on grounds of mental cruelty. Crooks didn't argue and the papers were signed within weeks. Not long afterward he was doing interrogations in Europe and she was engaged to the attorney.

Ana

Ana was trying to sleep. Tonight was the night she was supposed to help Gene and Ray leave Germany. The plan was for her to drive them up to Bonn where they would catch a train. She needed rest. Since Victor had come back she was finding it easier to sleep. His presence seemed to make the difference. Hopefully, he wouldn't be angry that she was leaving tonight, especially since she planned to be back by early morning. She rolled onto her side and closed her eyes. Her dreams had been so much better since Victor had returned. No more weird dreams about police or interrogations or Victor leaving. It sounded like it was beginning to rain. She lay there, hoping to doze off.

She thought about Victor. The last time they were in bed they were listening to Jimi Hendrix's album that included the song All Along the Watchtower. When it was over, she put on the Bob Dylan record with the original version of that song. Victor said he had never heard it.

"I love Bob Dylan," Ana had remarked. "He is my favorite. When he sings he sounds like a cat which carries a tune."

"How does it feeeeeel...?" Victor sang jokingly.

"Yes," replied Ana "That is what I mean. When he sings about being on your own in that song it is to make you see that you can do it. The characters are like a show of the unusual. Like a freak show. The song I really like on that album is the one about going back to New York City 'cause I do believe I've had enough."

Victor was playing around on an acoustic guitar he had found in the courtyard. He picked out the chords to "Wild Thing" and sang "You make my heart sing..." Ana joined in, the two of them leaning their heads together as if they were sharing a mike.

She fell asleep.

The apartment looked familiar. Ana lay on her side in a bedroom without windows. There was a Nepalese mountain coat over her. The other person in the room was a naked man who also seemed familiar. She felt like she was tripping and when she smiled at her bedroom partner, he smiled back. Leaning over her, he pulled the coat back, ran his fingers across her breasts and kissed her forehead The acid intensified and soon she and Karl—that was his name—were lost in a shared lust. The sex seemed to go on forever, his mouth on her legs, then her breasts, then her mouth. Her hands holding him, her mouth around his penis. Then the lust just disappeared and he reluctantly pulled away from her flesh. They began to talk. He told her he loved her while she remained quiet. He repeated his pledge; still Ana said nothing.

If I tell you something, he whispered, can you keep it to yourself? Ana smiled and said yes. This might be the information she wanted. I am a police undercover. I only tell you this because I love you and think you should know. Ana quietly ran her hand down his chest to his crotch where she lingered. His erection came back. She moved her head there. And waited for him to say more.

When her alarm sounded it was midnight. She remembered the dream and recoiled from the memory it evoked. Karl the narc; her sleeping with him to gain his trust and get information. The police raid with him pushing her off the fire escape once he realized what she had done. The episode was a part of her life she wished she could erase even if she had enjoyed the sex recalled in the dream. She got up and dressed quickly.

An hour later she, Gene and Ray were on the autobahn going north. Although it had been raining quite heavily when they left, it was dry now. There were a few puddles on the shoulder and that was it. Gene and Ray were sleeping in the back seat and Ana was going as fast as she dared. The plan was for the two men to take a train from Bonn to Hamburg and then take a ferry. Trains left every hour and a half so no matter when they arrived in Bonn there would not be a long wait. Ana was to stay with them until they were on the train. Then she would drive back to Frankfurt and wait for word from the deserter assistance people in Stockholm. Most of the people in her group had eventually come around. Although none of them wanted to use the group's name in the action, everyone but Ulf had individually lent their assistance. Some gave the men money while others made the necessary contacts along the route. Stockholm was expecting the two men.

Victor

Victor was at Roter Stern. He wondered where Ana was and couldn't remember whether or not she had said she had a meeting. Tired of waiting, he took out his vial of heroin and chased the dragon. Then he was out. He dreamed of milking cows with his uncle and smoking pot in the loft of the barn. He remembered the smell of the silage and the stench of the rotting manure. He recalled watching *Laugh-In* with his mom's boyfriends while they drank beer and whiskey and yelled at his mom to bring them more. He remembered the first day of boot camp and all the yelling and the fear. He recalled the fear of maybe going to Vietnam and the fear of dying and the fear of the army itself. Fear was what made the military tick. That held true for its soldiers and the people whose countries it invaded. Then he remembered singing in his uncle's church. Most of the songs were of the English tradition is what the choirmaster said but he also had them sing this really beautiful spiritual called "Wade In the Water." Then he was dreaming of Ana kissing him. He woke up, and found her next to him.

"Where have you been?" asked Victor groggily. His words were whispered and quite slurred. He pulled Ana close to his body. She kissed his forehead. Then she wriggled out of her pants and climbed under the sheets.

"I drove two GIs to Bonn to get them to Sweden." Ana took off his pants and began to play with him. He didn't rise even though he felt like he had an erection. It must be the heroin thought Victor to himself. He knew that he needed to call Crooks early in the morning to let him know about the desertion. Ana continued to play.

Victor stretched. He was getting stiff. "Something I always wondered was how people moved into these squats?"

Ana laughed. "That is, what do you say, a random question. I do not know exactly how Roter Stern got opened up, but the first one I was living in, we have gone in during the night. We have broken the lock on the gate and then we have climbed in windows. Then we have begun living there." She moved her mouth down his stomach.

The next morning they both woke before noon. Victor got up and began to pick out some songs on his guitar. He was playing a little solo he had made up in high school when he was teaching himself "Crossroads." Ana smiled as she pushed back the blankets.

"Robert Johnson." She said. "The American blues singer who died but no one knows how."

"Who?" asked Victor. "I only know this song from hearing Cream and Rory Gallagher play it.."

"Robert Johnson." answered Ana. "You silly Junge. The story has said he has sold his soul to the devil in trade for playing the guitar like nobody else. Many women have loved him. Some were other men's wives. They think maybe that is who has killed him. The song you are playing is about the railroad crossing where he has traded the devil his soul."

"They don't teach that in school."

Ana moved closer to Victor. She kissed the inside of his thighs. "I will teach you some other things you will not learn in school." Her hair covered his midsection. Victor caressed the small of her back.

Gene

Gene and Ray were on the train. Ray had calmed considerably. They were in Denmark and were sipping on some schnapps and enjoying the company of a couple Swedish women. The trip had been smooth as good whiskey so far. The last couple weeks had been a bit nerve wracking with rumors of the cops getting ready to bust the squats the men had been living in. One rumor even had their presence as being the reason for the busts. The rumors turned out to be bullshit. Gene figured they had been started by informers in the squatted buildings. Probably the same ones that sabotaged the defenses he had helped the squatters maintain. Despite the fact that the rumors were false, Gene and Ray had been moved by Ana to a sleazy hotel near the Hauptbahnhof for the last four days of their stay. Ray seemed fascinated by the comings and goings of the hookers and their johns. Gene had seen it all before. Growing up in the Market District of San Francisco with a pimp for a father meant he didn't have to leave much to the imagination when it came to street life. Beatings, junkies, getting laid at thirteen and cops. Lots of fucking cops.

"I think my friend Ray here grew up in suburbia," mused Gene. "Despite that he's got the right idea when it comes to race, especially for a white kid. He didn't have to throw that Molotov cocktail and make his life into what it's gonna' be from now on. Although if we keep meeting friendly Swedish chicks, it won't be that bad. At least until we get old and ugly."

After Denmark was Sweden. Ana had said that the most difficult border would be the German one and they had had no problems with their papers there. Both he and Ray slept during the ferry crossing.

Crooks finished his whiskey and motioned to the woman sitting on the barstool next to him. Although he was quite tired he was not going to let her go until they had some kind of sex. She gathered her purse and followed him into the hotel lobby. While waiting for the elevator she joked with him in German. In the elevator she stroked his crotch. By the time the door opened on their floor he was hard. It wasn't more than twenty minutes before she had serviced him, been paid, and left. Crooks fell asleep in his clothes, his pants unzipped. A call from the desk woke him three hours later. After showering, he fished around in his jacket pocket for a pill bottle. He took two de-soxyn, tossed them in his mouth and swallowed. On his way out, he paid his bill for another week. It was time to drive to the office.

Victor

Victor left the commune in the darkness before dawn. The sky was turning blue as he walked to a phone. He was heading away from the PX and toward downtown, having decided to go ahead with his plan to tell the ugly one about the deserters. Hopefully, it would get him off Victor's ass without getting Ana into any trouble. There was a phone a couple blocks away that was rarely used. He stopped at a Trinkhalle, bought some gum and asked for change. At the phone he put in twenty pfennig and dialed.

"Yeah?" It was Crooks' voice. Of course, thought Victor, why would he have any phone manners.

"Those guys are leaving this morning." Victor whispered into the phone.

"Are they driving or taking a train?"

"Both I think." Answered Victor. "Driving north and then catching a train up there somewhere. Bonn, Dusseldorf, I'm not sure."

"Thanks. I want to meet you later. Call me around 1600 hrs. tomorrow." Crooks hung up.

Victor hung up the phone and crossed his fingers.

The authorities would probably set up some kind of surveillance in train stations and alert the customs cops at the borders. The way he figured it the deserters should already be out of Germany, making it harder for them to get caught since supposedly no other country between here and Sweden tended to cooperate with the US military as much when it came to rounding up disenchanted GIs. He headed toward a Konditorei he knew of to buy some pastries for breakfast. Then it was back to bed with Ana.

Crooks got to work immediately contacting the German police and intelligence agencies he worked with. In turn, they would contact customs and the border cops. He planned to drive up to Bonn to check in with the Bundeskriminalamt and convince them to get the Danish and maybe even the Swedish officials on his side. Since it wasn't a straight-out desertion because of the war case, but involved actual criminal acts--the firebombings--maybe they would help him out. If not, he had other ways to track the punks down. He really wanted to arrest them, then let the Krauts have Willard. The Frankfurt cops would probably like to grab his girlfriend, too, maybe even more than Willard, given her history with them. What had that German told him? She had been involved in dealing LSD before she got into politics and escaped an arrest? The cops involved assumed she had convinced a narc she was sleeping with to let her know when the place she was living at was going to be raided. The undercover cop thought he had turned her and when he realized that she had used him, he tried to kill her. Even though the LSD had been confiscated, most of the suppliers had heeded her warning and avoided arrest. The undercover cop led the raid and said she had jumped out of a window to avoid arrest. Then she got into politics. A real firebrand at first, she wasn't afraid to fight the police. Since then she had not been as present on the street but there were apparently some German cops that wanted her ass. And, laughed the ugly one, what a nice little ass it was.

He headed for the parking lot and his car. As he was unlocking the door, one of the girls from the secretary pool yelled his name from the door of the building he had just left. He waved her over. She told him he was wanted immediately on the phone. Crooks went back inside.

"Hello." He answered.

"There's been another firebombing," came the voice at the other end. "We need you right away."

"Out at Höchst?" asked Crooks.

"Yeah. Somebody got hurt in this one."

Crooks hung up the phone and headed back out to the parking lot. It looked like there would be a delay to the start of his Bonn trip. He got in the car and started it. Hopefully, there were other CID out there to deal with the bulk of this new incident. When he got to the Höchst Kaserne, he drove straight in. The smell of smoke hit him when he rolled down his window to talk with the MP at the gate. The building that got torched looked like it had survived for the most part. Probably a fair deal of water damage but that was most of it. He parked and got out of the car. That long-haired Kraut undercover was there. Crooks wondered if maybe he had underestimated this guy. Maybe he was more than just another narco. If so, that probably explained his presence at this crime scene. After conversing with the uniformed MPs and a couple CID men, Crooks searched out the German. The person injured was a cleaning woman who had suffered some second degree burns and cuts when she tried to break down the door and escape the fire. The fire damage was limited to one room in the small one-story building. The water damage encompassed more than half of it.

Crooks found the German undercover. It was the long-haired individual from the first interrogation of Willard at the police station. The German nodded hello. He was taking notes in a small pad.

"Hello," said Crooks, extending his hand. "My name is Crooks. If I remember, yours is Karl? What have you found out?"

The two men shook hands.

"Ja, Karl. Not too much. It looks like an amateur job. Most of the gasoline splashed on the outside ground. We think the RAF has moved beyond this type of activity. They have more resources since they have started to rob banks. Would you like to compare information?"

Crooks, nodded. "I am going up to Bonn right now to track down a couple suspects. Would you like to come along?" The German said something to one of the other German cops and then motioned to the American that he was ready to go. The two men headed over to the car and got in.

After they were on the autobahn heading north, the German cop asked Crooks, "Is this information from your informant?"

Crooks nodded yes. "Two men wanted in connection with the earlier incidents at Höchst are supposed to be on a train going to the border on their way to Sweden. The informant overheard a conversation and said he made the men's acquaintance."

Do you know," asked the German. "That his girlfriend is involved with aiding Americans to desert the military?"

"I'm not surprised," answered the American. "I understand she has quite a history herself, yes?"

"She is responsible for the paralysis of a former partner of mine. . It was in a riot over the US military and Vietnam. She threw some bricks at the police lines when the order was given to clear the streets. One of those bricks hit my partner and paralyzed him. We couldn't prove it was her and her attorneys were very clever. Before that she had been living with some hippies that sold more than 300,000 doses of

LSD. Most of them got away because she warned them about the raid. She escaped from the building by jumping from a window. We had to arrest her several days later. She's been lucky. One day I...we will catch her!"

"You hate her, don't you?" asked Crooks. He could tell from the vehemence in the German's voice. He wondered if there was something more to Karl's story.

The German nodded yes. The American filed this information away.

Ana

Ana was sleeping when Victor returned, dreaming about walking in Rödelheim with her father. They would go to the river every Samstag and then to the Metzgerei for Wurst. After the Metzgerei, Papa would stop at a Gasthaus and drink a beer while Ana had Limonade. While Papa talked with the men in the Gasthaus, the owner's wife would give her pastries and the men would tease her. Hübschen, they called her. Papa was always so proud. The smell of the pastries Victor brought in woke her up. She smiled and took one. She didn't realize how hungry she was until she started eating. That evening she was supposed to go to a phone and make a call to Stockholm. Gene and Ray should meet their Swedish contacts this afternoon. Victor and Ana went back to sleep.

When she awoke it was late afternoon. Ana got dressed and headed out. There was a bar where she would make the call. She had plenty of time, so she decided to walk. While crossing a street near Eschenheimer Tor, a car ran a red light and nearly struck her. The driver yelled at her through the window while the passenger flashed what looked like a police identification card, as if to intimidate her. Ana continued on her way across the street, wondering what the incident meant. Winding her way through several back streets in case she was being followed, she ended up at the bar, ordered a beer and grabbed a copy of the Frankfurter Rundschau to read. The headlines were about an upcoming labor negotiation. On page three, there were a couple of paragraphs describing another firebombing incident on the Höchst Kaserne. Ana read the piece and wondered what the reaction was behind the scenes.

Time passed. Ana slowly drank a couple more beers. Then she went into the kitchen to make her call. After three rings she heard a voice on the other end.

"Allo?"

"Ist es der Stieg?" asked Ana.

"Ja," answered the voice. "Sie sind da. Wir haben ihnen getrafen um 22 Uhr."

"Alles ist gut?"

"Ja."

"Bis später." Ana hung up the phone. She thanked the bartender and left the building.

Tomorrow she would take her mother to church for the Stations of the Cross. Even though she was no longer a believer, Catholic ritual still intrigued her. As a teenager she accompanied her father to the Dom in Frankfurt for Easter Mass. She also recalled a performance of Beethoven's Missa Solemnis. The beginning of that Credo still gave her shivers. Her mother rarely even went to mass any more, but felt it was her religious duty to attend at least one Stations of the Cross during Lent.

Victor

Tarachi got a hold of me the day after I called the Ugly American and told me to meet him and his brother at the airport at a certain restaurant. I did and we headed back to the hotel we had been at before. After drinking a couple shots of ouzo Tarachi left, and it was just me and his brother. We waited around for a half hour or so until there's a knock on the door. It was two more Turkish guys. I'm thinking that these guys must be his mules or whatever you call the people that carry the dope over borders. The thing is, I don't think this is going over a border since opiates are cheaper in Turkey than in Germany. So maybe they run his distribution. Anyhow, Dean introduces the two guys and says their names are Ahmed and Muhammad. I go along with the introductions and we get down to business. They're putting up 5000 DM based on Tarachi's trust in me. We figured out a place to meet and negotiate about me having one other person with me. They say they have to think about it. I agree 'cause what else can I do? We set it up for five days from now. They're buying a fucking kilo of shit. I know I'm out of my league but I don't feel I got a choice. Maybe I can just leave everything behind once this deal goes down and the cops bust these cats. Ahmed and Muhammad shake my hand and tell me they will see me in five days at the Bockenheimer Warter Strassenbahn stop. They will be driving a Mercedes and will expect me to get into the car. Then we will drive to a particular park they know of in the Gastarbeiter part of town where we'll do the deal. I agree and shake their hands. Tarachi's brother reminds me that he's trusting me because of his brother and then he walks me to the hotel door, makes sure I get in a taxi and tells the driver to take me wherever I want to go. I tell the driver to take me to Sexy Sexy Sexy. He knows where it is, of course.

Once I got to the bar I called the German cop I was "working" with and he showed up about a half hour later with the long-haired narc that was with him and the Ugly American in the station. The narc said his name is Karl and that he's my partner from here on out. He told me he knew Ana and smiled a particularly slimy grin. I just hope for his sake that his cover is deep because I have a feeling that the guys I'm working with do their homework. It's not that I really give a shit what happens to the narc, but if they uncover his masquerade then I'm a dead man, too. While Karl and the other German cop bought me beers, they told me how the deal was gonna' go down. I told them about the plans me and the Turks had made to meet at Bockenheimer Warte and go from there. They nixed that straight out. They wanted an inside place they could wire. so now I have to see if the Turks had a place and then the Polizei would clear it and put some wiretap shit in the apartment I guess through a next door apartment.. They told me I was gonna' make the sale with Karl hanging out or there wasn't go be any deal. Once we walked away, the bust would be made. Karl and I would be arrested too and the pigs will make sure the Turks see us in the jail. That way Karl's cover won't be blown. I know they don't really care about mine. Now I gotta' go back to the Turks with the changes. I guess I hope they still wanna' do this. I find it ironic that the Ugly American's name is Crooks. He's still just the Ugly American to me.

Gene

So I'm walking down the street in some part of Stockholm two days ago. I'm by myself, seeing as how me and Ray decided it would be to our mutual benefit to split up. We made plans to check in with each other once a week at a certain coffee shop. So anyhow, I'm walking down this street and I start to feel like someone's following me. You know that feeling? It's not like they were obvious, but my street sense was telling me to try and lose whoever it was. So I turn left then right and so on but I still got that feeling. There's this black car in front of me just kind of keeping pace, so I start looking for an alley too narrow for that fucker to go down. When I find one I make a dash. I just keep running, winding down these alleys and sidewalks and through apartment buildings. Finally I lose the motherfuckers and I don't know where the hell I am. Fortunately, I still got a bunch of kroner in my pocket and I hide out until dark when I wander until I find some super sleazy hotel rooming house type place and rent a room for a week. While I'm there I hook up with this Swedish chick who's really a hooker and pretty damn nice and we get it on. She brings me food and vodka and whatever and I'm thinking I ain't never gonna' leave the place when I realize it's been almost a week and I should get a map or something so's I can find Ray tomorrow. She gets me a map and helps me figure out how to get to the coffee shop. When I get there there's no Ray. I wait a couple hours; I drank so much coffee I had to pee like a fuckin' racehorse. I finally decide he forgot and walk away. Just when I'm about ready to get on a bus one of the brothers who met us the first night we was in Stockholm appears beside me.

"Hey," he says. "Gene, right?"

"I nod my head yeah." What the fuck is goin' on I think.

"They picked up your partner." The brother is looking straight ahead the whole time like he's talking to a bird flying in front of him or somethin'.

"Shit." I say. "Who picked him up?"

"We don't know but we think it was the Embassy."

"You mean the US?"

He nods. ""Stay hidden wherever you at. We'll find you if we need to. Something got fucked up somewheres."

He gives me a little dap and walks away. Now I'm real paranoid and decide not to take the bus. I began winding my way through the streets and alleys again wondering if I should go back to that chick. I decide I might as well. It's been three days since that happened. This chick, her name is Olga, shaved my head and I'm growing a beard but being black in Stockholm a man is gonna' stand out no matter what. Good thing I like Olga.

Ana

The meeting was one of the best attended meetings in at least a year. Every single person who had ever been involved with the group seemed to have made it. Church members, political people, SPD and their youth branch the Jusos, even the pastor of the Anglican church that sometimes steered GIs their way and always gave the group money whenever they asked. The call had been responded to beyond anyone's hopes. The only question on the table was suspending the activities of the group concerning assisting deserters. Ana and Janns were on the hot seat.

"So, because two members ignored my warning we are in this trouble." That was Ulf. He sure did take it personal, thought Ana.

"I do not think it is right to criticize our members." said an older woman that had donated the money to put Gene and Ray up at the hotels they had stayed in after leaving the squats. The majority of the group nodded in agreement.

"May I speak?" It was Janns. He went ahead. "Ana and I took it upon ourselves to help the two men out of the country. We felt that they deserved our assistance since it was plain that the American police wanted to arrest them. As any student of American Rassismus knows, their lives were threatened. It is true that they committed a criminal act. However, they did it for political reasons. This is a difference."

"Violence is violence." said Friedrich.

"We respect your views and those that agree with you," continued Janns. "That is why Ana and I accepted the consensus opinion and did this action as individuals."

"You are fortunate that the GIs have not been picked up." said Friedrich.

"May I remind you," this from the Anglican pastor, "we are always lucky that the GIs do not get picked up." Many of the group members nodded thoughtfully.

"That is true." agreed an older woman who had opposed helping Gene and Ray on pacifist grounds. "I also understand that this was not an action that had our approval and that Ana and Janns did this on their own. However, in the climate of today mit the RAF committing many violent acts in the name of the left and the revolution we cannot risk our name and future."

"I propose that we suspend our operations." Ulf looked around as he said this. Most were nodding their heads in agreement.

"Should we make an announcement?" asked the

pastor. "If we don't then how will the public know we are not involved with the firebombings should the authorities try to link us to them?"

"That would only happen if they were told by one of the men who deserted," said Janns.

"Or if an informant said something." That was from a university student whose primary role in the group was finding places for deserters to stay in the university community while they waited for preparations to be completed. He had been very helpful when Gene and Ray needed a place. His comment dropped like a lead balloon.

"I move that we do both." said the older female pacifist that had spoken before. A vote was taken and passed. Chores were divided up and the deserters assistance committee was no more. Ana and a few of the other members headed to a coffee shop to socialize. She was upset about the way the meeting had dissolved, as were the members she was with now . Those who were not afraid of the police resolved to figure out another vehicle to carry on their work.

Crooks

After riding with the undercover named Karl I started asking around about him. Turns out he's been running undercover for years. So long in fact that he could probably never be a regular cop again. Hell, he probably could never be a regular person again. I've seen undercovers become their disguise. In a way it makes sense since you never get to be yourself, especially if you don't have a regular life to go back to every once in a while. According to some of the other Kraut cops, Karl is real good at what he does but it seems like he creeps a few of them out. Like any cop he's got a couple, three questionable occurrences on his record. You know, unwarranted use of the gun, police brutality and so on. The thing is Karl's got two killings on him that were never resolved. That's a little unusual, but then there's a period he spent on paid leave so that he could dry out. According to this other Kraut I been working with he wasn't drying out from alcohol but from methamphetamine. I started asking around about the LSD bust Karl told me about on the ride to Bonn and, after being brushed off several times I finally found someone who worked with him on that case.

He told me Karl had the suppliers dead to rights. He had made several buys, had met the people closest to the manufacturer, and was close to bringing down the entire operation. That's when that girl who is now Willard's girlfriend entered the scene. Some of the dealers in the LSD operation were growing suspicious of Karl and had finally convinced themselves to stop selling him any drug until they found out who he was working for. It seems that they began to wonder why the product they were selling him was never appearing on the street. I mean these people were selling enough so that the fact those pills were not on the street was noticeable. That girl volunteered to seduce Karl into thinking he was using her while in reality it was the other way around. Word was Karl fell in love. That's when she turned the screws and found out about the raid. The original plan was for her to be gone when the raid occurred, but Karl was forced to move the timing up. The only druggies busted were that girl and one fellow who was sleeping in the bathtub. She ran to escape and ended up near a window. Karl was the only cop in the room. She told him what a fool he was, and further emasculated the dumb ass. Then, depending on who you want to believe, she jumped out a window in the room when he started beating her or he pushed her out the window while he was beating her. She ended up landing in a dumpster full of paper, got up and got away for a couple days. The cops tracked her down and arrested her a couple days later. The Kraut who told me this story said Karl never forgot not only how he was used but how much he was in love. He's the kind of man that probably only had one love in his life.

Victor

Victor was on his way to the house in Oberursel to meet up with Crooks. He hoped his plan had worked out; that the GIs were safe in Stockholm with the ugly one believing he somehow missed them despite his best efforts. If Crooks wasn't convinced Victor's information was genuine, Victor knew he was in for some trouble. Then he would have to think quickly. The streetcar was near the end of the line in Oberursel. It was almost time to face his lies and hope they worked.

He waited for Crooks. There was an American MP standing guard in fatigues and a helmet. He stared at Victor, probably wondering who the hell he was. When Crooks entered the room, the MP left. He stood in front of Victor.

"Your information was incorrect."

Victor said nothing and waited.

"I want to assume that you thought you were giving me something timely but you know what happens to people that assume—"

Victor shifted in the chair he was sitting. His left

leg had fallen asleep.

"However," Crooks spoke again. Victor watched his jaw move. It was amazing how square it was. With his crew cut the guy looked like the offspring of a muscular J. Edgar Hoover. His jowls hung down like a basset hound and he had a big mole on one side of his face. Victor thought how scary he would look to someone high on LSD. "Our people arrested one of those fellows in Sweden, so I am not going to pursue that line of questioning. I figure we'll get the next one, too. What I am going to do, though, is ask about the latest firebombing incident in Höchst. Have you heard anything about that?"

Victor hadn't. He said as much. It didn't look like Crooks believed him.

"I expect you will." said the ugly one. "You have my number and I will expect a call once you hear. Meanwhile, I hear your drug dealing is meeting with some success."

Victor said nothing. He waited while Crooks took off his jacket and placed it on a chair in the room.

"You know, " began Crooks. "That your new friend Karl slept with your girlfriend?"

There was no reaction from Victor. He didn't believe the cop. Crooks smiled.

"I have proof," he continued. "Do you want to see it? Or I could bring your new friend Karl in here."

This guy is such a fuckin' asshole, thought Victor, but what if he's tellin' the truth?

"From what he tells me, your girlfriend helped him bust a big LSD ring a few years ago."

Victor found this hard to believe. Ana wouldn't work for the cops, no way.

Victor left the house. He wished the whole thing would just go away. Sometimes one action led to another but switching gears could make it into something positive. He didn't see how the road he was on could end up any way but worse than it already was.

Louisa poured her husband a bourbon. The couple sat in the living room of their quarters relaxing after the Colonel's return from the States. On the ride back from the airport, Louisa had mentioned Porgy's visit.

"I don't understand why you invited him here." said the Colonel.

"My daughter is seeing him and I want to meet who my daughter is seeing." Louisa responded. She didn't tell her husband Martha was probably sleeping with the young man. The Colonel was not in a very receptive mood.

"I know you are aware of the rules against fraternization across ranks." He continued.

"That's not what this is about." Louisa replied. "Besides, you did not fraternize with him, did you?"

"I don't want my daughter wasting her life over some man or his politics.. She's been accepted to Yale for Christ sake. Teenage passions rarely last, you know that." The Colonel was close to losing his cool. Louisa wondered whether she should push the issue.

"What," she asked, bristling. "Is the problem with Porgy? His rank or his origins?"

"Now you know," the Colonel responded. "I don't care about his origins."

"Damn right you don't," said Louisa. "We all come from the same chains and quarters mister. They were selling all of our grandmamas and grand-daddies. Let me remind you that none of us are far from our history no matter what we done to improve ourselves. Hell, you know that--."

Both heard the doorknob turn. Martha was home. They ended their argument unresolved, just like they always did. Arguments were frowned upon in the family

At the Record Store

Martha and Porgy were on the Opernplatz, enjoying the good weather and each other. There was a small record shop in an alley behind the Opernplatz that carried obscure albums, including an entire section of jazz and rock bootlegs. Porgy had only recently discovered the place while wandering around on his day off. This first visit he spent 100 DM on two bootlegs of Miles Davis at a show in Sweden and three obscure European issues of some old Big Bill Broonzy. It was also the only place he knew that carried the kind of needle he liked for his turntable.

Martha watched Porgy look through the record bins. It reminded her of how she probably looked when she was in a bookstore. The music playing in the store was the latest from Sly and the Family Stone. The song playing was "Luv and Haight," a sing-songy, mildly funky tune about the reduction of the counterculture into a junkie scene of ugliness and despair. Looking out the window while Porgy shopped, she thought she saw Victor heading their way. It had been quite a while since she had seen him. Porgy hadn't mentioned him in a while either. He looked like he was doing okay. A little furtive maybe, but she supposed that was to be expected since he was essentially a fugitive. He entered the store.

"Hey," he seemed surprised to see Martha. "How you doin'?"

Porgy looked up from the record bin he was thumbing through.

"Hey man, how's it goin'?" asked Porgy.

"I'm okay. I didn't know you knew about this place."

"Yeah," responded Porgy. "I found it a few weeks ago when I was just wanderin' around. Good stuff." The guy at the counter nodded towards Victor.

"I been coming in here for a year or so." He waved hello to the salesman.

"Martha, right?" asked Victor. Martha nodded yes.

"Good to see you," she said. Victor joined Porgy in thumbing through the bins, hoping to find a copy of a Rolling Stones bootleg he had read about in a recent issue of *Oz*, the underground paper from Britain. Supposedly, it included some songs from the Frankfurt show he had attended. That was some show. The police dogs almost tore his pants leg off on the way in. The set they played was heavy on stuff from *Let It Bleed*. Mick Taylor and Keith

Richards had quite a guitar-playinig interaction going at that show. Victor was convinced Taylor's playing brought Keith to greater heights than the previous guitarist Brian Jones ever had, especially that night.

Martha told Porgy she was going outside. The two men made their purchases and left the shop. Victor found the Stones bootleg and Porgy bought a Last Poets disc he had never heard. Once outside, they stood idly, wondering what to do next.

"You guys doin' anything?" asked Victor. "I've got nowhere to go." He was calmer now than he had been at the house in Oberursel.

"I could do with some food," answered Martha. The men agreed and the three of them headed for the Wimpy's burger place near the Hauptwache. They ordered burgers and fries, found a table and ate. Martha went back for a milkshake. While she waited for her order at the counter, Porgy decided to be direct.

"You doin' that heroin, Victor?"

Victor looked up. He knew that he should lie but he couldn't.

"Just a little," He had a packet in his pocket that held at least a quarter gram.

"Does Ana know?"

Victor shook his head no. Porgy thought about whether he would say anything more. He decided not to.

"You know Porgy ..." Victor looked at Porgy, his eyes trying not to blink. "When I was in high school I used to think of saying fuck it but something always prevented me. My uncle's kindness, some chick I had the hots for, my friends, shit even my mom. Lately though, I find myself ready to go ahead and not give a shit about anything and just let the fuckin' chips fall wherever they might."

Porgy remained quiet. He shook his head and looked away. Then, he turned back to Victor. "That was your conscience talking, fool." Porgy had seen this before with those brothers in Oakland who thought the Panthers were bullshit and the only thing to live for was the street and the next high or fuck. It wasn't pretty.

Martha was back with her drink and the three hung around while she sucked the ice cream through a straw.

"What music did you get, Victor?" Martha asked, making conversation.

"Oh, some Rolling Stones." He took the album out of the shopping bag and handed it to her. Martha looked at the cover. It featured a grainy photo of Mick Jagger and some writing that looked kind of like illuminated manuscript, except it was solely in black type.

"I like some of their stuff." She looked inside the cover where the songs were listed. "That song "Sympathy For the Devil" has a great percussion part. And I love that line about cops and criminals and all the sinners bein' saints. Some guy at school said the Stones were listening to a lot of Last Poets when they made that album. Maybe that's where they got the percussion idea from."

"Maybe." Victor remembered the Last Poets album being in a scene in *Performance*. The day was turning cloudy outside. Martha was stroking Porgy's thigh under the table.

"We gonna' go in a couple minutes," said Porgy. He gathered the trash from the meal and took it to a wastebasket. The three left the restaurant and headed toward the Strassenbahn stop.

"See you around?" asked Porgy as he shook Victor's hand.

"I don't know man, I'm busy these days."

"Oh yeah?" Porgy looked up. "Doin' what?"

"You don't wanna' know. I'm kinda' crossed up about some shit."

"Watch your ass, bro," said Porgy. "And don't get my girl Ana into any shit she don't wanna' be in. You been dealt some bullshit, but you ain't the only one." Martha and Porgy headed across the tracks to wait for their streetcar. Victor headed toward the U-Bahn station. He waved goodbye to Martha.

Martha was curious. While they waited for the Strassenbahn, she peppered Porgy with questions.

"That last statement was pretty cryptic, Porgy. What the hell did you mean by it?"

"Nothing." answered Porgy. "That boy is sinking down to places you don't wanna' know about."

"I can take it." Replied Martha. "You should tell me and maybe I can help."

Porgy hesitated. He wasn't sure Martha needed to know about Victor's habit.

"Come on, brother," teased Martha. "I'm a big girl. Is he into some bad drugs or something? I've seen that before. Hell, there's a friend at the high school whose brother is strung out on heroin."

"I'm thinkin' he has some company in Victor," said Porgy.

"Are you goin' to tell Ana?"

Porgy hesitated. It was a question he didn't want to answer. "I don't know."

"How can you call her a friend and not tell her?"

Porgy knew Martha was right. "I don't know that it's my place to tell her."

"That's bullshit," responded Martha. "You can put yourself out for someone you don't even know like Angela Davis, but you won't let your friend know her boyfriend is hooked on dope?"

"Shit, Martha…It ain't like that."

"Yeah it really is." Martha backed off a little. She didn't want Victor's problems to get in the way of her growing relationship with Porgy. "Besides, his actions put her and her political groups at risk."

Porgy remained silent. He walked a bit ahead of Martha while considering her words.

Victor

Things are some fucked up. I ran into Porgy a week or so ago and hung out with him and his chick. That was all right but I know Porgy ain't no fool. He knows I been doing more than just chipping on the heroin. He told me before that he saw guys so strung out in Nam that they couldn't remember how to shoot their carbines and that was something you wanted to remember over there. Either that, he said, or they didn't care enough about their life to save it. I think that's closer to where I'm at right now. I've been hanging with Ana every other night or so but everything is lukewarm again. I've been playing the guitar more, though. That's all right. Nothing fancy but learning a lot of chord progressions and some modal stuff. If I wasn't on the lam I would see if I could sit in with a band, but I just don't know what's gonna' happen to me.. Two weeks until the Grateful Dead show.

Right now, I'm riding the Number 13 streetcar downtown. It's time for me to meet up with the two Turks again. As they say, the deal is going down.

*Karl is coming with me. I hope they don't mind —
otherwise who knows what the cops have planned
for me. Prison is the most likely scenario. Here's
Opernplatz, my stop. And there's Karl. The guy is a
weirdo. I guess going undercover either appeals to a
certain kind of freak or makes you one. Anyhow,
let's see how it goes.*

Victor got off the streetcar and started walking
south. Karl fell in next to him. He was wearing one
of those coats from India or Nepal that were big
with the German hippies. They were made from goat
or sheepskin with a border of some kind of fur
around the bottom, front and hood. Most of them
have some kind of embroidery. Karl's did. It looked
pretty worn in and smelled like hashish just like the
ones worn by real hippies.

"Did you tell the buyers when to meet?" asked
Karl.

Victor nodded yes. As it turned out, the cops
were not cool at all with the way he and the Turks
had set up the deal. There was no way they wanted
to meet them in a public place and get into their car
with the dope. Karl was not going to go along with
that plan at all. After another meeting where Karl
laid out the plan, Victor contacted Tarachi's brother
and let him know the new details. He hesitated at
first but the price and the quality of the dope was
too good a deal to pass up. They agreed to set up the
meeting in an apartment Tarachi's brother kept on

Altkoenigstrasse. Victor figured he used it when he wanted to party and bring in hookers or whatever he was into. After another meeting with Karl, who had the police check out the apartment and then approve it as a good enough place to make the arrest, Victor contacted his buyers. They were supposed to be there already and the German cops were ready to bust in as soon as they heard the deal go down. The whole place had been wired by the Germans. Victor was still against meeting anywhere that could be wired, but the Germans insisted and it wasn't like he was in a position to negotiate. Karl and Victor were outside the building. It was modern like most of the buildings downtown, especially those near the Opernhaus. The Americans had destroyed most of Frankfurt in their bombing raids during the war. For some reason they really seemed to have it in for the Opernplatz area. Victor pushed the security buzzer near the outside door and was let in. Although the Turks were told that Karl was the seller and was coming with him, the Turks remained concerned with his presence. Victor's thought was that the worst that could happen is that they refused to deal.

The apartment was on the third floor. The door was unlocked and Karl and Victor walked in. No guns were obvious although Victor was pretty sure there were some on the Turks' bodies. The apartment was very nicely furnished. Velvet curtains, velvet divans whatever they are called. Mahogany and teak tables. The Turks asked them to sit down and poured four glasses of ouzo.

"This is Karl," Victor said by way of introduction. Karl shook their hands.

"Ist er der Mann mit dem Produkt?"

"Ja."

They drank another glass of liquor. They were small glasses, kind of like shot glasses only a different shape. One of the Turks took out a briefcase from underneath the divan. He unlocked the case and showed the money. Karl asked Victor to count it, then pulled out a small brick wrapped in paper and inside a larger glassine bag. It was the heroin. He set it on the table in front of him and unwrapped it while Victor finished counting the money.

"Alles ist da." Victor told him.

Karl pushed the heroin across the table and one of the Turks took a pocket knife out of his pocket. He scraped a small amount of the heroin from the brick and put it on his tongue then made a face due to drug's bitterness.

"Es ist die gleiche wie vorher." He told the other Turk. The two men wrapped up the heroin and put it in the briefcase.

"Sie müssen hier fünf Minuten warten," said the Turk who had tasted the drug. They left the apartment. Like a small army, five or six German cops in uniform ran out of the next apartment and stopped the Turks in the hall. While most of the cops arrested the Turks, cuffing them and so, two came into the apartment and did the same to Karl and Victor. They took them all down the stairs and into the street. By the time they were in two waiting cars, a fair-sized crowd had gathered. Karl and Victor went in one car and the Turks went in another. Victor never saw the Turks again.

Karl spoke rapid German to the driver of the police car. He told him to take us to the address in Oberursel. Back to the fuckin' Ugly American again. I am so tired of his ugly face. To top it off his breath usually smells like salami and cat shit. Not easy to breathe when his face is six inches away. I'm guessing it's part of his intimidation strategy. Someone else will have to be the judge of how well it works. I'm hoping that he didn't find out I bullshitted him on those deserter guys.

Victor was back in the same room as before in the Oberursel house. No MPs were present. It seemed to be just him, Karl and the ugly one. He was sitting in the same chair as before and Crooks was pacing back and forth in a rather agitated way. After what seemed like an eternity to Victor, he finally sat down in a chair opposite Victor in a classic cop pose with the chair turned backwards. He pulled a cigar out of his shirt pocket and lit it. That was something new, thought Victor, dreading this enhancement to the ugly one's already foul breath. He tried to hold his breath, although he knew there was no point. To begin with there were no windows in the room and even if there were, they would remain closed.

"So," began Crooks. "You helped the Krauts get their drug bust. That counts for some brownie points with them, but not with me or my boss. You know what we want and it doesn't have much to do with drugs. We want the fucking firebugs who are trying to burn down Höchst and we want them before some other asshole revolutionaries get the idea that it's okay to burn down barracks."

He inhaled deeply on the cigar and then exhaled the smoke directly into Victor's face. Victor turned away and coughed.

"I'm surprised the smoke bothers you," said the ugly one. "What with the hash you all smoke. That stuff smells a hell of lot worse than this cigar which was given to me, by the way, by that nigger colonel in charge of race relations. You know he hates that job. He would be just as happy as me to put you and your friends, no matter what their color, in Leavenworth. It drives him crazy that his daughter is hanging out with one of them nigger radicals. I think you know who I am talking about."

Victor didn't like where this was going. He had no desire to get Porgy or his girl involved in his bullshit.

"Don't worry," continued Crooks. "We are just watching that situation right now. We're not asking you to do anything until the colonel's daughter leaves for college. Then we'll get your nigger friend before he gets out of the service. He's slick but he thinks we play fair."

From his interaction with the ugly one, Victor knew that playing fair was pretty far back on the cops' list of preferred strategies, especially in the military where GIs had no rights to speak of. The CID pretty much had the power to do whatever the hell they wanted. Of course, that worked in his favor, too. Otherwise, he would probably be in prison already, but as long as they needed him and he acted like he could help them he was able to stay on the streets. The leash they had him on could be yanked in at any time and he knew it. He just hoped he figured out a way to disappear before that occurred. Karl entered the room, waved the cigar smoke away from his face and offered Victor a bottle of Limonade and a Brotchen with butter. Victor thanked him and ate hungrily. While Victor sipped on the Limonade, Karl pulled a chair over and sat.

"You have helped," he said to Victor. "But you are not finished helping."

"That's more than I can say about this little prick." remarked Crooks. Karl laughed.

"Now, you must help us arrange a deal mit the hashish seller to the Zoom Club dealers." Karl leaned back on the chair. Victor said nothing. "We have determined that there is one major supplier for the men and girls that sell hashish in that club and at the Jazzkeller. Because the Jazzkeller is a respected place we will not make arrests there. We do not like the Zoom Club and want to close it up. You will help us or we will give you back to the Americans for prison."

This stunk, thought Victor. They probably knew he dealt occasionally at Zoom; that he sold mostly to GIs and moved a few ounces a week. He didn't know how close he was to the main supplier.. He had no desire to bust these people. They were almost like friends. He got high with them almost every day and hung out where they lived and drank.

"We will use a plan similar to the one we have just completed with the Turks and heroin except you will be the buyer, ja?" Karl ran his fingers through his long and somewhat greasy hair. He certainly looked the part of a German doper.. "Because you have the Kontakten this should be no problem I think. I will give you two weeks to make the arrangements. You will ask to buy at least ten kilos and you will insist on meeting the main seller, verstehst du?"

Victor nodded his head yes. Ten kilos and two weeks. He needed to get the hell out of Dodge. Maybe he could get the Germans to front him the cash and just split. What the hell difference did it matter now?

Karl was traveling in a car with the two Turks on the autobahn headed towards Freiburg. The Turks figured they were going to be transferred to Turkish authorities at the next border but Karl had other plans. However, after Freiburg, they continued south. One of the Turks asked to use a restroom. Karl pulled off the autobahn, found a small restaurant, and pulled into the restaurant parking lot to oblige. Before he got out of the car he turned to the Turks.

"I know you wonder what is going on," he said.

They nodded.

"I know you work for a very big businessman in Turkei, ja?" asked Karl.

The Turks nodded again.

"I am not interested in him. I understand that there will always be heroin and drugs." Karl smiled. "So, I think it is better if men like your boss sell the drugs instead of scum like the hippies or the blacks. I am going to take you to a train station. You will get on the train and go back to Ankara. There will be police on the train. They will not be in uniform. They will follow you to Ankara. They will get information from you. When I need your help you will come. Okay?"

The Turks nodded again. The three men went into the restaurant and ate. Afterward, Karl brought them to the train station, returned their passports to them and made sure they got on the train. The undercover police followed the Turks on. They would probably even sit in the same compartment.

Lunch

Porgy and Martha were meeting Ana for lunch. The ostensible reason for the meeting was to catch up on Angela Davis news and the preparations for the upcoming rally in June. Porgy figured he would talk about Victor, too. They were meeting at the coffee house down from Roter Stern. Porgy bought some cold cuts and Brotchen, pastries and coffee. He and Martha waited for Ana. He hoped Ana would act as if there were nothing between them. He really did not want Martha to know.

"My father comes back tomorrow," said Martha. They had spent the last two nights together with the consent of Martha's mom. After the dinner with Porgy she gave the go ahead. Martha had asked about her father's reaction and Louisa said she would deal with him "You should meet him."

Porgy hesitated. He didn't want to hurt this girl's feelings but neither did he want to meet her dad. "Someday, babe. Some day." He put his hand between her thighs. Martha smiled and let loose a quiet sigh. Ana came in the door of the restaurant, saw the two and smiled. Once again she was wondering where Victor was. It had been a couple nights since he had been at the commune.

The three of them hugged each other in greeting. Ana ordered a pot of coffee. While they waited for drink, Martha started talking.

"You heard they acquitted two of the Soledad Brothers, didn't you?" Martha was bordering on ecstatic.

"Ja. I saw that. And Angela dismissed the prosecution's attempt to say she did it all for love..."

"Yeah." Porgy interrupted. "I'm thinking that she may actually get off."

"What makes you say that?" asked Martha.

"Just a feeling. Mostly because an all-white jury let off them two brothers."

"That is a hopeful sign." agreed Ana. She was thinking about whether or not Angela could have done it all for love. Was an intelligent woman likely to allow her emotions to affect her decisions? She couldn't answer that question. If she reflected on her situation with Victor, it could be said she was allowing her love to make questionable decisions. She doubted that Angela had been motivated only by her feelings for George Jackson. The waitress set the coffee pot on the table. Ana thanked her and poured each one at the table a cup.

"I saw a small article in the *New York Times*

about their reporter covering the trial," said Martha. "He got arrested for marijuana possession. I don't want to be conspiratorial, but maybe the cops didn't like how he was reporting the lies of the prosecution?"

Ana finished her first cup of coffee and poured another, motioning to the waitress for another pot. Porgy searched for an opening.

"Ana," he began. "I don't want to put my nose in your business but…"

"Are you going to ask me about Victor?" she had expected he would be a topic of this conversation. "I have not seen him in two days."

"We saw him a few days ago," Martha told her.

"Yeah" added Porgy. "We had a hamburger with him."

"And talked about music." Martha reminded him.

"Yeah. Music and some other stuff."

"What kind of other stuff?" asked Ana.

"Well…" Porgy hesitated. "I don't know what to say, but he told me he was on heroin."

"I have been afraid of this," said Ana. She looked into her coffee cup, small tears welling up in the corners of her eyes. A combination of anger, fear and sadness crept into her face. "I do not know what to do. I cannot make him leave because I love him. Because I love him I want to help him, but I am not in this part of his life and do not know how."

"There must be a free clinic that would help," thought Porgy aloud. "They must deal with addiction among the runaways and hippies. I know they do in the States."

"Natürlich....see, my thinking is not clear. Danke," said Ana. "They will know how to help."

"Let us know if we can help," Martha smiled at Ana. Ana nodded, finishing her cup of coffee. She stood. Martha and Porgy did the same, hugging her in turn. As she watched the two of them walk away, Ana realized that Martha did not know about her and Porgy.

Victor

Victor figured he had been in jail for five days. There was no calendar that he could see, nor were the jailers very helpful when he asked them the date or time. If he had counted correctly, though, he had eaten thirteen meals. That made it the fifth day of his incarceration, which would make it May Day. He had yet to get a visit from any kind of cop, including Karl or the Ugly American. His biggest concern was what had happened to Ana. They were walking to the coffee shop on Eschersheimer Landstrasse the morning of April 26th when the bust went down. Two uniformed German cops and Karl pulled their car to the curb and got out. Karl walked in front of them and the two other cops came up behind. Ana started to run and they grabbed her. Before Victor could do anything, he was on the ground and being cuffed. They pulled a gram of heroin from his pants pocket and showed it to Ana. Then, another car pulled up and each of them were shoved into different cars.

It had all begun when he was released after the

Turks got busted. After a couple days in the Oberursel house, he began to set up the hashish deal. It was more complicated than he thought it would be. There was some concern from the supplier's people because of his recent bust. The deal had never been completed, seeing as how Karl busted him and Ana two days before it was supposed to go down. A weird thing about the bust is that Karl gave him a packet of heroin once he was in jail, which he had rationed out in such a way so he would not get sick.

The jail he was in was not the same as where he was taken in his previous arrest. Victor guessed it was like the German version of a county lockup. The next level after the city jail, so to speak. The cell was clean and he was the only one in it, but he could talk with the other prisoners around him. There was even a television, which seemed to be controlled by the guards. Right now it was off. The food was okay. He felt terrible about getting Ana busted. She had nothing to do with his drug habit. He should never have let her take him in. Like King Midas in reverse, everything he came in contact with turned to shit.

Crooks waited for Karl in the director's office of the prison where Victor was being held. The director of the prison was talking to him about the RAF and the string of bank robberies they had pulled off in recent months. The ugly one listened half-heartedly. He was concerned about the RAF but figured it was primarily a problem for the Germans. His focus was on getting the Höchst firebugs off the street and making sure that Victor got his just desserts. All he was looking for was a dishonorable discharge and a few months in Leavenworth. That would show the punk how things really were. Crooks assumed Karl and the Germans were through with Victor and ready to give him back. He watched through the window as Karl parked his car and walked up the stairs to the director's office.

Once Karl was sitting in the office, the director left the two men to talk.

"So," began Karl. "The attempt to arrest the hashish dealers has failed. I do not think your American deserter can be of any more use to me. Do you want him?"

Crooks smiled then cracked the knuckles of his massive hands. "Ja." "Then he is yours. However, please do not move him until all of the paperwork is done. We can make that last two or three weeks. He is okay in this prison."

"Sure."

"I mean," continued Karl. "There is no problem with jurisdiction."

"I do not think many people even know that he is here." said Crooks.

"This is good, then." smiled Karl. "I will let you know when the transfer papers are ready."

The two men shook hands. Karl left the office

and the ugly one sat back down. He wanted to see Victor, but needed the director's permission.

Victor heard somebody coming. The footsteps echoing in the corridor were coming closer. They stopped outside his cell. He waited until the thick metal door was opened. There stood the ugly one and a German official. After thanking the official, Crooks walked into the cell, and sat on the bunk. Victor moved away, trying to make a comfortable space between him and the Ugly American. The ugly one offered him a cigarette. Victor took it and waited until the ugly one lit it.

"I'm guessing," began Crooks, "that you know your girlfriend is in prison. She is being charged with possession of heroin and aiding and abetting arson." This was a lie, but Victor had no way of knowing. No charges had been filed on anyone in that case. A little intimidation was always effective in getting what the Ugly American wanted from criminals.

"That's bullshit," Victor knew she was set up. "She never touched heroin. If she knew I was using she would have left me."

"Prove that." Crooks knew he had the upper hand. No policeman, judge or even regular citizen would believe that someone living Ana's lifestyle would not use heroin. The common understanding did not make distinctions between hippies, hashish smokers, squatters and real drug addicts. Or left wing rioters, for that matter.

Victor took another drag on the cigarette. It tasted like a real American Marlboro. He had been smoking HBs for so long he had forgotten what American cigarettes tasted like. "I don't think she was involved with the firebombings either. She is against arson."

"You can help her." Crooks smiled. It was particularly menacing.

"By ratting on someone?" Victor was derisive.

"How did you guess?" Crooks stood up. He paced the small dimensions of the cell. His huge body made it look even smaller than it was. "I want to know what you know about Porgy Johnson and the Höchst arsonists."

"Nothing. Porgy wouldn't go there. That's all I know."

Crooks had a request from the Colonel to get any information on Porgy that he could. It was the ugly one's impression that Victor was probably telling the truth. Porgy Johnson seemed like he was too smart to get involved with a couple of firebugs who were pissed at their CO. But, a colonel's request is a colonel's request even if the colonel was a Negro. He had to make an effort.

"Look," Crooks leaned into Victor's face. There was the terrible breath again. He grabbed Victor's hair and yanked it hard and did not let go. When he did he pulled several strands of hair from Victor's head. Then he punched Victor in his gut. "Give me something."

Victor leaned over, trying to catch his breath. The ugly one punched him again. Some cops preferred psychology, but plain violence had always worked for him.

"Give me something."

"Porgy is not involved," insisted Victor. "Neither is my girlfriend. Why don't you just fucking believe me?"

The ugly one pulled Victor's head back, yanking his hair again. He punched Victor in the mouth. Victor spat out blood and what felt like a piece of a tooth.

"Fuck you!" He spat again. Crooks pushed Victor down onto the bunk and turned toward the cell door. After leaving the cell he closed the door. On his way out of the prison, he stopped in the director's office and told him he should send a medic to Victor's cell.

Ana

What was Victor doing? Was he on heroin all of the time? I have been asking this question ever since I was in the police car. The police took me to a prison I believe is still in Hesse. It is hard for me to know because I have no communication with any-one but the jailer. She tells me nothing. It is very clean and seems to be modern. At least it is not a medieval prison like many in Deutschland. I keep thinking about Victor and perhaps how stupid I was being with him. This is why guerrillas do not like fighters to be in love. The lovers do not see security problems with their love even when they might be obvious to others in the cadre. Maybe I should have had a casual relationship with Victor like I have with Porgy.

It must be five days since I was arrested. I have not heard any charges, but I believe I am being ac-cused of heroin possession. The police that arrested me planted a small amount of powder on me and produced it when they were booking me at the sta-tion. I know that it was not mine but what can I say? I have asked for an attorney but have heard nothing. I think that this is unusual. However, I am essentially powerless in this prison. I would like to have a book to read and to be able to contact someone who would go see my Mutti. I was planning to visit her in two more days.

There is nothing to do here. I cannot sleep any more.

She thought about Victor. And Porgy.

Karl had an appointment with a prosecutor. He hoped to convince him to bring charges against Ana for the attack on his partner in the earlier riot. Failing that, he figured he could get a charge of possession. When the deserter that was suspected of the firebombings was returned to the American authorities in Frankfurt, Karl hoped to tie Ana to that case, too. Knowing the American was not shy in his use of violence during interrogation, he figured the deserter would say whatever he was told. If not, Ana's knowledge of the arson might be enough to charge her as an accessory. Karl wanted her put away and did not care how he accomplished that goal. He would never forget her making a fool of him. Whatever they might be, charges had to be filed in the next twenty-four hours to be within the limits of the law. Today was May first. She was arrested April 26th. If the May Day protests in the streets today got out-of-control Karl might not get a chance to talk with the particular prosecutor he was going to see. That would limit his chances for getting anything serious against Ana, since only this prosecutor knew her history, thereby making it more likely he would go along. Upon entering the Justice Building in downtown Frankfurt, Karl headed to the elevator, pushed the button and went up to the prosecutor's office. Outside, the noise of the protest grew louder as the march and came nearer. He found the office, entered the anteroom, said hello to the receptionist, sat down and waited.

"He is ready." The receptionist spoke to Karl as the prosecutor opened the door to his office.

"Allo Karl." The two men shook hands. The prosecutor had been the official that encouraged Karl to go undercover after the riots that injured his friend. Both men shared a conservative view of the world that favored the Adenauer government over anything Willy Brandt and the SPD might put together. If they were to choose a politician whom they could support in the Germany of 1972, it would be Josef Strauss, the ultraconservative Bavarian. Karl pulled up a heavy oak chair and sat down. The prosecutor picked up a sheaf of papers from his desk and began to read.

"Ana Becker arrested for possession of heroin, April 26, 1972. Arrestee had one-half gram of heroin in her possession when picked up on Eschersheimer Landstrasse the morning of April 26, 1972 at approximately 1030 Uhr. She was apprehended with an American soldier who was absent without leave from his unit and is a known narcotics seller. Fräulein Becker was brought to Frankfurt Polizei station near Hauptwache. She was booked and transported to Frankfurt Two prison where she is currently being held." He stopped reading and looked at Karl. "Why are you interested in this case, Karl? It is a typical possession case. Is this Fräulein Becker a prostitute? Let someone else handle this. I understand you are still working undercover on some narcotics and political cases. I have spoken with the ministers involved and they do not want you to end those investigations."

Karl spoke softly and firmly. He set his hands on the desk.

"Hans," he began. "This is Ana Becker. You must remember her from earlier. In 1970 we were ready to arrest several men in the Bockenheimer district with many thousands of doses of LSD. Becker escaped from our officers out the window and down the fire escape. In 1970 she was in a riot against the Amis. Several officers were injured in that battle, including my partner. I cannot let her go back to her life. She is under investigation by the security services in Bonn for her political activities. She may be part of the Rote Armee Fraktion, although no evidence ties her to them. The American military CID wants her out of business because she has helped GIs to desert their military service. She is connected to the black radicals who were put in prison last year. The Americans think she worked with the Black Panthers in the military to burn the barracks in Höchst. I can---"

The prosecutor interrupted Karl. "I understand Karl. This is about revenge for you. I am sympathetic. However, I do have a question. If Fräulein Becker is such a political person, then why was she arrested for heroin? These leftists and anarchists do not usually involve themselves with drugs like that." Hans sat back in his chair, waiting for Karl's explanation. He anticipated exactly what he heard.

"I had my men plant the drug on her when we took her from the street," answered Karl. "I knew that she was much too clever to get arrested for her political activities. Her boyfriend and his drug addiction is her weak link. I will drop the drug charge when you have charged her with the crimes she is guilty of."

The prosecutor was silent. He was hesitant to stretch the law as much as he was being asked to but he also sympathized with Karl's desire to put Fräulein Becker in prison for many years. If she were released there was a good chance she might disappear. It seemed that there was quite a network of like-minded individuals who would eagerly shelter her for as long as necessary. He stood and began to pace, then he stopped.

"I will allow her to stay in prison for two more weeks. Charge her with possession and if there is not enough evidence to charge her with crimes we know she is suspected of, she will be released. You have already violated procedure and the law by holding her without any charge for this long. That gives us until May 14." He folded his hands as if in prayer. "You must allow her to see an attorney. It is okay if you make her wait a few more days before that occurs."

Karl stood up and shook the prosecutor's hand. Hans showed him to the door.

Porgy

I'm very concerned. I ain't seen Ana in five or six days. She wasn't at the Angela meeting last night. Last I heard she and Victor were going to a Dead concert at the Jahrhunderthalle in Höchst. Shit, I was with her a couple days before that concert. We talked about our sexual thing and Victor. She said things were cool and Victor didn't seem to know or if he did, to care. Shit, I never seen her miss a meeting.

I ain't seen Victor either. God knows what that boy is up to. I saw him one time after the day we went to Wimpy's. That was near the Zoom Club. I was coming out of an apartment building near there, it was getting on to evenin' and I looked over to see Victor talking to three maybe four German hippie looking guys. It looked like they were smoking some dope and having a hard time keeping the pipe lit. I walked over to say hi and they all stopped talking. Victor was kind of short with me but still polite. He didn't do no introductions but that's understandable. I'm guessing they were talking about a drug deal which is why they shut up so quick. So I walked

away. I went up into the club but he never came in
so I gave up and went back to the barracks.

Ana

It was May 3rd. Ana had finally heard her charges. She was right. The charge was possession of heroin. She contacted a friend who had in turn contacted an attorney. They were meeting in an hour. The guards were permitting her to take a shower before seeing him. She was familiar with the attorney from the Hausbesetzung movement. He had defended several of the squatters on charges of assault when the police attacked them in the front yard of an estate in Westend.

I feel much better after the shower. The guards have taken me to a room where I will meet the attorney. Right now I just feel good to be out of the cell. This room has a window where I can see sky.

The door opened and the attorney entered. He extended his hand. "Allo, Ana."

"Allo, Josef." He sat in a chair opposite Ana and pulled a notebook from his briefcase. After the guard left the room and closed the door, Josef made certain it was secure. Then he sat back down.

"What happened?" he asked. "I did not expect that you would have drug charges against you."

"The drugs were planted," said Ana. "I was arrested on the sidewalk when my boyfriend and I were walking to a coffee shop. The police jumped out of a car and arrested us. I thought at first they were after my boyfriend, but then they cuffed me too and put me in another car. When I got to the first jail they searched me and produced a packet with powder in it. I guessed it was heroin. I do not know where it is from. I never have even seen the stuff up close and have never used it."

Josef wrote down her story. "I understand. They have manufactured the drug charge so they can keep you in jail since they have no other charges. Who is your boyfriend?"

"He is an American GI who has deserted the military. His name is Victor Willard. I have been told by a mutual friend that he does occasionally use heroin."

"Why would you be with him?" asked Josef. "This is a security risk for your political work."

"I did not think he carried heroin with him," answered Ana. "And I love him."

Josef nodded. Love and politics was a volatile mix. In his experience they could rarely mix for too long. One commitment would eventually destroy the other. He was convinced that politics had the longer shelf life.

"Can you tell me more about this man Victor?"

"I met him at the Speyer rock fest in October. He was looking quite unkempt when he sat down next to my camp late at night. I think it was Saturday. We spent the night talking and keeping warm. We smoked some hashish and drank wine. He told me his story. He was AWOL because a sergeant in his unit had been attacked in self-defense by a friend of his. His friend is a black man and the sergeant was a racist white man. They had argued before. Victor was afraid for his life so he left the next day once the MPs released him. He was living on the streets and keeping hidden. When I met him at the rock festival he had not bathed for many days and was hungry. I took him back to the Roter Stern to help him get healthy and we fell in love. He is not a politically minded person like me. He prefers to hang out in the Zoom Club and smoke hashish. He plays guitar. Do you know the GI named Porgy?"

Josef nodded his head yes. Porgy was one of his favorite people. They had worked together during the Ramstein Two case and Josef had been impressed with Porgy's intellect and maturity.

"He warned me that Victor was –how did he say—in over his head. I thought I could help him. Then when I knew I couldn't, I was too much in love with him to make him leave. We were going to a Grateful Dead concert the night of April 26th and then we got arrested."

"Ja." smiled Josef. "The Grateful Dead. I enjoy their music. Our office was responsible for their legal contracts with the promoter. I actually met some members of the group. Pleasant and articulate young men, especially for Americans."

"Victor would like that," Ana said to herself as much as to anyone else. "Can you find out where he is?"

"First," began Josef. "I will try and get this heroin possession charge on you dismissed. Then I will try to find this Victor. If I cannot get your charge dismissed, I will try to get you out of jail until a trial or other resolution is found. Are you being treated well?"

"It is okay." Said Ana. "I would like to have a newspaper and some books."

"I can arrange that." Josef smiled. He shook Ana's hand. She smiled back. Josef rapped on the door and the guard let him out. Then Ana was escorted back to her cell.

Karl

It was May 13th. The action in police stations, prisons and other structures related to law enforcement in the Bundesrepublik was in overdrive. This was true in both German and US facilities. Ever since the explosions at the IG Farben building in Frankfurt two nights earlier the entire security apparatus of both governments had been on high alert. Still, the bombers were able to destroy fifty police vehicles at the Bundeskriminalamt building in München the following night. The case against Ana, which was weak to begin with, had been pushed aside in favor of the more immediate reality of the RAF.

Karl refused to let it drop, though. He had obtained the paperwork for her transfer the day before. Doing so was easier than he anticipated, probably because of the concentration on the RAF. After borrowing a police undercover car -- a Mercedes 300SL, in fact -- he drove to the prison. He parked the car, crossed the parking lot and entered the building. He already knew where Ana's cell was located. Once he provided the paperwork to the jailer and got his signature, he walked through a door unlocked electronically by the guard and headed toward her cell. He entered the cell, cuffed her and walked her down the corridor, out the door and to the car. No one asked him where he was going. The fact that that most prison guards were acting as policemen manning traffic stops on the autobahn in the wake of the RAF attacks made his task easier. He started the engine and pulled away into the street. He knew exactly where he was taking her: to Bockenheimer Landstrasse, from Bockenheimer Landstrasse he turned left onto Schlossstrasse towards Rödelheim. He took another left on to Rödelheimer Landstrasse and drove slowly through Rödelheim. Ana was strangely quiet.

"What are you doing?" she finally asked. "Where are you taking me?" The situation didn't seem quite right. After the bombing of the IG Farben Building and the American Officers Club, her attorney had told her to expect being moved to a more secure prison but there were no prisons in Rödelheim. As far as she knew, there were no prisons in this part of Frankfurt. Maybe some small jails for drunks but no prisons. The car continued on Rödelheimer Landstrasse to Westerbachstrasse and out towards Höchst.

Karl looked in the Mercedes' rear view mirror and smiled grinned at her confusion. After traveling three or four kilometers on Westerbachstrasse he took a left, then slowed down to a crawl and drove a few hundred meters. Next, he pulled the car onto a dirt trail that led into what looked like a deserted orchard. The trees were full of buds and blossoms, cherry blossoms. The Mercedes continued moving down the overgrown trail. Perhaps five hundred meters from the road, Karl stopped the car. They were completely hidden from the road. From what Ana could tell there were no inhabited buildings for at least half a kilometer in any direction. Karl turned around.

"Kennst du mich?" He asked. Ana shook her head no. She did not recognize this man. Karl didn't believe her.

"LSD arrest. 1970."

Ana looked again. A glimmer of recognition quickly morphed into a complete memory of that night in 1970. She remembered Karl as the narc she slept with in order to get information; whose conversations after sex revealed information that saved a number of her friends from arrest and years of prison.

"You!" She shouted. She struggled to move but the seat belt and cuffs were too tight for her to do much of anything but grunt in exasperation.

"Please." whispered Karl. "Not so loud."

"What do you want?"

"Do you remember?" Asked Karl. "You ran from me when we arrested your friends. I told you I would catch you, and now I have."

"You tried to kill me," answered Ana. He had pushed her off the fire escape but she had landed in a trash bin. At the time she had laughed because the fall and landing seemed like something from a television show. The trash had probably saved her life. She lay in it for at least an hour after Karl left. All she suffered were some sore muscles.

"You may not know this, but it was you who paralyzed my partner last year." Karl reached into the Mercedes' glove compartment and retrieved a pistol. Ana was puzzled.

"What?" she asked.

"When you and your friends tried to storm the PX last spring, you threw bricks at us police. One hit my partner and he went down. He has never walked again."

Ana considered what the Polizist was saying. She remembered the protest now. It was possible that she had thrown the brick he was talking about, although the odds seemed almost impossible. She had been in a few battles with the cops that day. Still, she didn't remember ever hitting one, even if she wanted to. Her arm just was not that strong.

"I think you are wrong," she said, hoping to calm Karl, although she feared her attempt was useless. "You must have me confused with someone else. Besides, we weren't trying to storm the PX. You and your fellow police attacked us after we stopped in front of it and began to sit down to block the street. Lots of people were throwing things."

"That is not how it happened. Wouldn't you remember the person who hurt your friend?" Karl got out of the car. He opened the rear door, unbuckled the seat belt and pulled Ana from the car. "Do not try to run. You will be shot. No one can hear us here." He put the gun in Ana's back and pushed her further into the underbrush. Thorns tore her pant legs. They pushed their way through the brush for another hundred meters to a small clearing. There was a small concrete structure like a chicken coop in clearing, perhaps five meters by five meters. The roof was pretty dilapidated and the outside paint on the blocks was well worn. Karl grabbed Ana by the arm and dragged her into the building. Blood streaked the walls.

"I did not try to kill you in that LSD arrest. You ran and fell." Karl pushed Ana to the floor. There were small piles of some kind of animal dung all over the floor. "I went into the room where you were hiding and tried to grab you. You went out the window to the fire ladder. When I went toward you, you fell. If I wanted to kill you, I would have."

"Scheisse! That's a lie." yelled Ana. "You grabbed me on the fire escape. I pulled away because I didn't want to touch you anymore. That's when you pushed me and I fell two stories. You were angry because I used you. We ran undercover on you instead of the other way around. You left me for dead, you schwein. If I had landed on the street I would be dead. I just got lucky when I fell in that trash bin. The landing was on papers and not something like metal or nails."

"I should have double-checked and made sure you were dead.

"I see," said Ana. She understood. "You are the fool who would think I would love you. Since you could not kill me you want to discredit me, to keep me from talking. You are afraid I will destroy your career. I do not care about your career! You arrested me for a junkie so people will not believe me if I tell them about your illegal actions. Your sleeping with informants. Your skimming money from the drug dealers. You trying to kill me. You think it was easy for me to fuck you? You are a schwein.. Fuck you. I don't care if you are crooked because the system you work for is too. Why should you be different?" She no longer cared. Her anger and hatred of this cop had taken over. Karl kicked Ana in the crotch several times. She gasped for breath while moving away from his foot.

"You do not think there are honest Polizisten?" Asked Karl, shouting. "My friend was honest."

"Your friend was as brutal as you." Ana spit at Karl. "What difference does it make if there are honest pigs when the system is a crooked scheme?"

Karl hit her with the gun across the face, drawing blood. Then he began to kick her head. Ana wondered who would tell her Mutti. She stopped struggling, unconscious. Karl put the pistol to her head and pulled the trigger. The blood began to ooze from under her head where it lay on the dirty floor. He crouched over the body, careful not to get blood on his clothes and shoes. After dragging it out of the building into the woods, Karl deposited the corpse in a shallow grave he had dug earlier. Then he covered it with dirt and brush. until he was satisfied it could not be seen. The relative remoteness of the site made it unlikely the corpse would be found for weeks. In addition, a prevalence of carnivorous small animals would probably render the corpse harder to identify if it was discovered. Then he left the orchard, covering his tracks as he did so. After getting back in the Mercedes, he drove back to Frankfurt using a roundabout way through Höchst then Schwannheim and into Sachsenhausen. There, he parked the Mercedes and walked to the river where he tossed the gun after wiping it for prints. He went to a small Gasthaus he knew in the district and drank several glasses of Apfelwein before returning the Mercedes. Tomorrow he would try to visit the American boyfriend.

Martha

"There must have been ten thousand protesters, Porgy!" Martha was trying to talk quietly. Most of the people at the tables around them were military and quite nervous about any kind of protesters because of the IG Farben bombings a few days earlier. "We got to some intersection near the river and a Strassenbahn pulled into the center and stopped. Just stopped. Then rows and rows of pigs started moving in from the other three directions. It was like they wanted us to run so they could beat us up. Then they turned on the water cannon. That was freaky. It just scooted people across the road tearing big holes in their pants and everything…"

Martha and Porgy were in the PX cafeteria. It was May 17th. Her father was back at the Pentagon on temporary duty again. There had been protests in Frankfurt against the US mining of the northern Vietnamese harbors for more than a week. Porgy had stayed away while Martha had attended as many as she could without missing school. She was enjoying the rush, especially after seeing the police unleash the water cannons. Her secondary reason for attending was to see if she could find Ana or Victor. The best she had been able to do was to talk to a couple of Ana's friends that Martha knew from her Angela Davis work. It might be time to visit Roter Stern. The possibility existed that one of them might have heard something. However, the commune was being watched twenty-four hours a day by a variety of security and police agencies. According to the news media, the police were quite certain that some members of the RAF were hiding in Frankfurt. Naturally, the Roter Stern was considered a potential hideout, along with every other squatted house.

All military Kasernes and facilities were under lockdown because of the IG Farben bombing. The Germans had set up checkpoints at random places in the city and at almost every autobahn exit. Every vehicle entering an area where Americans either worked or lived was subject to a search. MPs used mirrors on extended handles to look under cars for bombs. Identification was demanded at every door to every US facility. Most GIs were working sixteen hour shifts with eight hours off. Porgy had so far been able to escape that regimen. He was reading the *Frankfurter Rundschau* and Martha had a copy of the *Stars and Stripes*. The news was almost entirely about the RAF and their attacks. The most recent one had been on a judge who was responsible for signing the warrants against the group. His wife had been badly injured. The newspapers cried for blood, especially the *Stars and Stripes* and the rightwing German rag *Das Bild*.. Even though Martha and Porgy understood the political reasons behind the bombings, the killings and injuries hit a little close to home. On top of that was the fact that the bombings provided the authorities with an excuse to crack down hard on the Left.

Porgy scanned a series of smaller articles inside the section that dealt mostly with Frankfurt city news. He found a small piece, perhaps three or four column inches that described the death by suicide of an American GI in a German prison facility. The article stated that the man, whom, according to prison officials was named V. Willard, was found hanged in his cell. He had used a piece of bedding to do the deed. The article continued, saying that the prisoner was imprisoned on April 26 for possession of heroin. Because he was a citizen of the US, the American Embassy had been contacted. Then it was discovered that he was an AWOL GI. He was waiting for transfer to the US authorities when he died. It was unknown, said the article, why he had been in German custody for more than two weeks.

Porgy read the article twice, wanting to make sure that he was translating the German correctly. When he was convinced it said what he had first read, he showed it to Martha. Even though her German skills were not as good as Porgy's she understood the article. Neither said anything. They both wondered what had happened to Ana. Neither felt good about the possibilities.

Fomite

Burlington, Vermont

Fomite is a literary press whose authors and artists explore the human condition—political, cultural, personal and historical—in poetry and prose.

A fomite is a medium capable of transmitting infectious organisms from one individual to another.

"The activity of art is based on the capacity of people to be infected by the feelings of others." Tolstoy, *What is Art?*

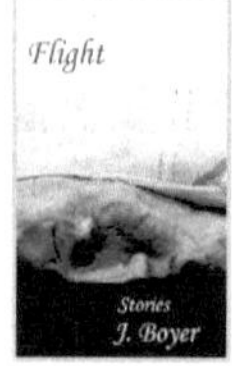

Flight and Other Stories - Jay Boyer

In *Flight and Other Stories,* we're with the fattest woman on earth as she draws her last breaths and her soul ascends toward its final reward. We meet a divorcee who can fly for no more effort than flapping her arms. We follow a middle-aged butler whose love affair with a young woman leads him first to the mysteries of bondage, and then to the pleasures of malice. Story by story, we set foot into worlds so strange as to seem all but surreal, yet everything feels familiar, each moment rings true. And that's when we recognize we're in the hands of one of America's truly original talents.

Loisaida - Dan Chodorokoff

Catherine, a young anarchist estranged from her parents and squatting in an abandoned building on New York's Lower East Side is fighting with her boyfriend and conflicted about her work on an underground newspaper. After learning of a developer's plans to demolish a community garden, Catherine builds an alliance with a group of Puerto Rican community activists. Together they confront the confluence of politics, money, and real estate that rule Manhattan. All the while she learns important lessons from her great-grandmother's life in the Yiddish anarchist movement that flourished on the Lower East Side at the turn of the century. In this coming of age story, family saga, and tale of urban politics, Dan Chodorkoff explores the "principle of hope", and examines how memory and imagination inform social change.

Improvisational Arguments - Anna Faktorovich

Improvisational Arguments is written in free verse to capture the essence of modern problems and triumphs. The poems clearly relate short, frequently humorous and occasionally tragic, stories about travels to exotic and unusual places, fantastic realms, abnormal jobs, artistic innovations, political objections, and misadventures with love.

Fomite
Burlington, Vermont

Loosestrife - Greg Delanty

This book is a chronicle of complicity in our modern lives, a witnessing of war and the destruction of our planet. It is also an attempt to adjust the more destructive blueprint myths of our society. Often our cultural memory tells us to keep quiet about the aspects that are most challenging to our ethics, to forget the violations we feel and tremors that keep us distant and numb.

Carts and Other Stories - Zdravka Evtimova

Roots and wings are the key words that best describe the short story collection, *Carts and Other Stories,* by Zdravka Evtimova. The book is emotionally multilayered and memorable because of its internal power, vitality and ability to touch both the heart and your mind. Within its pages, the reader discovers new perspectives and true wealth, and learns to see the world with different eyes. The collection lives on the borders of different cultures. *Carts and Other Stories* will take the reader to wild and powerful Bulgarian mountains, to silver rains in Brussels, to German quiet winter streets and to wind bitten crags in Afghanistan. This book lives for those seeking to discover the beauty of the world around them, and will have them appreciating what they have—and perhaps what they have lost as well.

When You Remember Deir Yassin - R.L. Green

When You Remember Deir Yassin is a collection of poems by R. L. Green, an American Jewish writer, on the subject of the occupation and destruction of Palestine. Green comments: "Outspoken Jewish critics of Israeli crimes against humanity have, strangely, been called 'anti-Semitic' as well as the hilariously illogical epithet 'self-hating Jews.' As a Jewish critic of the Israeli government, I have come to accept these accusations as a stamp of approval and a badge of honor, signifying my own fealty to a central element of Jewish identity and ethics: one must be a lover of truth and a friend to the oppressed, and stand with the victims of tyranny, not with the tyrants, despite tribal loyalty or self-advancement. These poems were written as expressions of outrage, and of grief, and to encourage my sisters and brothers of every cultural or national grouping to speak out against injustice, to try to save Palestine, and in so doing, to reclaim for myself my own place as part of the Jewish people." Poems in the original English are accompanied by Arabic and Hebrew translations.

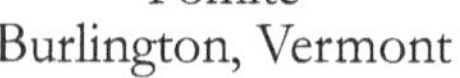

The Co-Conspirator's Tale - Ron Jacobs

There's a place where love and mistrust are never at peace; where duplicity and deceit are the universal currency. *The Co-Conspirator's Tale* takes place within this nebulous firmament. There are crimes committed by the police in the name of the law. Excess in the name of revolution. The combination leaves death in its wake and the survivors struggling to find justice in a San Francisco Bay Area noir by the author of the underground classic *The Way the Wind Blew: A History of the Weather Underground* and the novel *Short Order Frame Up*.

Short Order Frame Up - Ron Jacobs

1975. America has lost its war in Vietnam and Cambodia. Racially-tinged riots are tearing the city of Boston apart. The politics and counterculture of the 1960s is disintegrating into nothing more than sex, drugs and rock and roll. The Boston Red Sox are on one of their improbable runs toward a postseason appearance. In a suburban town in Maryland, a young couple is murdered and another young man is accused. The couple are white and the accused is black. It is up to his friends and family to prove he is innocent. This is a story of suburban ennui, race, murder and injustice. Religion and politics, liberal lawyers and racist cops. In *Short Order Frame Up*, Ron Jacobs has written a piece of crime fiction that exposes the wound that is US racism. Two cultures existing side by side and across generations--a river very few dare to cross. His characters work and live with and next to each other, often unaware of the other's real life. When the murder occurs, however, those people that care about the man charged must cross that river and meet somewhere in between in order to free him from (what is to them) an obvious miscarriage of justice.

All the Sinners Saints - Ron Jacobs

A young draftee named Victor Willard goes AWOL in Germany after an altercation with a commanding officer. Porgy is an African-American GI involved with the international Black Panthers and German radicals. Victor and a female radical named Ana fall in love. They move into Ana's room in a squatted building near the US base in Frankfurt. The international campaign to free Black revolutionary Angela Davis is coming to Frankfurt. Porgy and Ana are key organizers and Victor spends his days and nights selling and smoking hashish, while becoming addicted to heroin. Police and narcotics agents are keeping tabs on them all. Politics, love, and drugs. Truths, lies, and rock and roll. *All the Sinners, Saints* is a story of people seeking redemption in a world awash in sin.

Fomite
Burlington, Vermont

The Listener Aspires to the Condition of Music
- Barry Goldensohn

"I know of no other selected poems that selects on one theme, but this one does, charting Goldensohn's career-long attraction to music's performance, consolations and its august, thrilling, scary and clownish charms. Does all art aspire to the condition of music as Pater claimed, exhaling in a swoon toward that one class act? Golden-sohn is more aware than the late 19th century of the overtones of such breathing: his poems thoroughly round out those overtones in a poet's lifetime of listening."
John Peck, poet, editor, Fellow of the American Academy of Rome

Visiting Hours - Jennifer Anne Moses
Visiting Hours, a novel-in-stories, explores the lives of people not normally met on the page—-AIDS patients and those who care for them. Set in Baton Rouge, Louisiana, and written with large and frequent dollops of humor, the book is a profound meditation on faith and love in the face of illness and poverty.

Roadworthy Creature, Roadworthy Craft - Kate Magill
Words fail but the voice struggles on. The culmination of a decade's worth of performance poetry, *Roadworthy Creature, Roadworthy Craft* is Kate Magill's first full-length publication. In lines that are sinewy yet delicate, Magill's poems explore the terrain where idea and action meet, where bodies and words commingle to form a strange new flesh, a breathing text, an "I" that spirals outward from itself.

The Derivation of Cowboys & Indians - Joseph D. Reich
The Derivation of Cowboys & Indians represents a profound journey, a breakdown of The American Dream from a social, cultural, historical, and spiritual point of view. Reich examines in concise detail the loss of the collective unconscious, commenting on our contemporary postmodern culture with its self-interested excesses, on where and how things all go wrong, and how social/political practice rarely meets its original proclamations and promises. Reich's surreal and self-effacing satire brings this troubling message home. *The Derivations of Cowboys & Indians* is a desperate search and struggle for America's literal, symbolic, and spiritual home.

Fomite
Burlington, Vermont

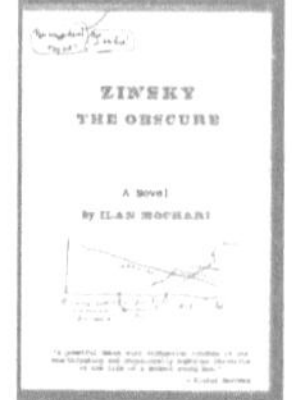

Zinsky the Obscure - Ilan Mochari

"If your childhood is brutal, your adulthood becomes a daily attempt to recover: a quest for ecstasy and stability in recompense for their early absence." So states the 30-year-old Ariel Zinsky, whose bachelor-like lifestyle belies the torturous youth he is still coming to grips with. As a boy, he struggles with the beatings themselves; as a grownup, he struggles with the world's indifference to them. *Zinsky the Obscure* is his life story, a humorous chronicle of his search for a redemptive ecstasy through sex, an entrepreneurial sports obsession, and finally, the cathartic exercise of writing it all down. Fervently recounting both the comic delights and the frightening horrors of a life in which he feels—always—that he is not like all the rest, Zinsky survives the worst and relishes the best with idiosyncratic style, as his heartbreak turns into self-awareness and his suicidal ideation into self-regard. A vivid evocation of the all-consuming nature of lust and ambition—and the forces that drive them.

Kasper Planet: Comix and Tragix - Peter Schumann

The British call him Punch, the Italians, Pulchinella, the Russians, Petruchka, the Native Americans, Coyote. These are the figures we may know. But every culture that worships authority will breed a Punch-like, anti-authoritarian resister. Yin and yang—it has to happen. The Germans call him Kasper. Truth-telling and serious pranking are dangerous professions when going up against power. Bradley Manning sits naked in solitary; Julian Assange is pursued by Interpol, Obama's Department of Justice, and Amazon.com. But—in contrast to merely human faces— masks and theater can often slip through the bars. Consider our American Kaspers: Charlie Chaplin, Woody Guthrie, Abby Hoffman, the Yes Men—theater people all, utilizing various forms to seed critique. Their profiles and tactics have evolved along with those of their enemies. Who are the bad guys that call forth the Kaspers? Over the last half century, with his Bread & Puppet Theater, Peter Schumann has been tireless in naming them, excoriating them with Kasperdom....
from Marc Estrin's Foreword to Planet Kasper

Fomite
Burlington, Vermont

Raven or Crow - Joshua Amses

Marlowe has recently moved back home to Vermont after flunking his first term at a private college in the Midwest, when his sort of girlfriend, Eleanor, goes missing. The circumstances surrounding Eleanor's disappearance stand to reveal more about Marlowe than he is willing to allow. Rather than report her missing, he resolves to find Eleanor himself. *Raven or Crow* is the story of mistakes rooted in the ambivalence of being young and without direction.

Views Cost Extra - L.E. Smith

Views that inspire, that calm, or that terrify—all come at some cost to the viewer. In *Views Cost Extra* you will find a New Jersey high school preppy who wants to inhabit the "perfect" cowboy movie, a rural mailman disgusted with the residents of his town who wants to live with the penguins, an ailing screen writer who strikes a deal with Johnny Cash to reverse an old man's failures, an old man who ponders a young man's suicide attempt, a one-armed blind blues singer who wants to reunite with the car that took her arm on the assembly line— and more. These stories suggest that we must pay something to live even ordinary lives.

The Empty Notebook Interrogates Itself - Susan Thomas

The Empty Notebook began its life as a very literal metaphor for a few weeks of what the poet thought was writer's block, but was really the struggle of an eccentric persona to take over her working life. It won. And for the next three years everything she wrote came to her in the voice of the Empty Notebook, who, as the notebook began to fill itself, became rather opinionated, changed gender, alternately acted as bully and victim, had many bizarre adventures in exotic locales and developed a somewhat politically-incorrect attitude. It then began to steal the voices and forms of other poets and tried to immortalize itself in various poetry reviews. It is now thrilled to collect itself in one slim volume.

Fomite
Burlington, Vermont

The Good Muslim of Jackson Heights - *Jaysinh Birjépatil*
Jackson Heights in this book is a fictional locale with common features assembled from immigrant-friendly neighborhoods around the world where hardworking honest-to-goodness traders from the Indian subcontinent, rub shoulders with ruthless entrepreneurs, reclusive antique-dealers, homeless nobodies, merchant-princes, lawyers, doctors and IT specialists. But as Siraj and Shabnam, urbane newcomers fleeing religious persecution in their homeland discover there is no escape from the past. Weaving together the personal and the political *The Good Muslim of Jackson Heights* is an ambiguous elegy to a utopian ideal set free from all prejudice.

Travers' Inferno - *L.E. Smith*
In the 1970's churches began to burn in Burlington, Vermont. If it were arson, no one or no reason could be found to blame. This book suggests arson, but makes no claim to historical realism. It claims, instead, to capture the dizzying 70's zeitgeist of aggressive utopian movements, distrust in authority, escapist alternative life styles, and a bewildered society of onlookers. In the tradition of John Gardner's Sunlight Dialogues, the characters of *Travers' Inferno* are colorful and damaged, sometimes comical, sometimes tragic, looking for meaning through desperate acts. Travers Jones, the protagonist, is grounded in the transcendent—philosophy, epilepsy, arson as purification—and mystified by the opposite sex, haunted by an absent father and directed by an uncle with a grudge. He is seduced by a professor's wife and chased by an endearing if ineffective sergeant of police. There are secessionist Quebecois involved in these church burns who are murdering as well as pilfering and burning. There are changing alliances, violent deaths, lovemaking, and a belligerent cat.

Suite for Three Voices - *Derek Furr*
Suite for Three Voices is a dance of prose genres, teeming with intense human life in all its humor and sorrow. A son uncovers the horrors of his father's wartime experience, a hitchhiker in a muumuu guards a mysterious parcel, a young man foresees his brother's brush with death on September 11. A Victorian poetess encounters space aliens and digital archives, a runner hears the voice of a dead friend in the song of an indigo bunting, a teacher seeks wisdom from his students' errors and Neil Young. By frozen waterfalls and neglected graveyards, along highways at noon and rivers at dusk, in the sound of bluegrass, Beethoven, and Emily Dickinson, the essays and fiction in this collection offer moments of vision.

Fomite
Burlington, Vermont

My God, What Have We Done? - Susan Weiss

In a world afflicted with war, toxicity, and hunger, does what we do in our private lives really matter? Fifty years after the creation of the atomic bomb at Los Alamos, newlyweds Pauline and Clifford visit that once-secret city on their honeymoon, compelled by Pauline's fascination with Oppenheimer, the soulful scientist. The two stories emerging from this visit reverberate back and forth between the loneliness of a new mother at home in Boston and the isolation of an entire community dedicated to the development of the bomb. While Pauline struggles with unforeseen challenges of family life, Oppenheimer and his crew reckon with forces beyond all imagining.

Finally the years of frantic research on the bomb culminate in a stunning test explosion that echoes a rupture in the couple's marriage. Against the backdrop of a civilization that's out of control, Pauline begins to understand the complex, potentially explosive physics of personal relationships.

At once funny and dead serious, *My God, What Have We Done?* sifts through the ruins left by the bomb in search of a more worthy human achievement.

As It Is On Earth - Peter M. Wheelwright

Four centuries after the Reformation Pilgrims sailed up the down-flowing watersheds of New England, Taylor Thatcher, irreverent scion of a fallen family of Maine Puritans, is still caught in the turbulence.

In his errant attempts to escape from history, the young college professor is further unsettled by his growing attraction to Israeli student Miryam Bluehm as he is swept by Time through the "family thing"—from the tangled genetic and religious history of his New England parents to the redemptive birthday secret of Esther Fleur Noire Bishop, the Cajun-Passamaquoddy woman who raised him and his younger half-cousin/half-brother, Bingham.

The landscapes, rivers, and tidal estuaries of Old New England and the Mayan Yucatan are also casualties of history in Thatcher's story of Deep Time and re-discovery of family on Columbus Day at a high-stakes gambling casino, rising in resurrection over the starlit bones of a once-vanquished Pequot Indian Tribe.

Fomite
Burlington, Vermont

The Housing Market - *Joseph D. Reich*

In Joseph Reich's most recent social and cultural, contemporary satire of suburbia entitled, "The Housing market: a comfortable place to jump off the end of the world," the author addresses the absurd, postmodern elements of what it means, or for that matter not, to try and cope and function, and survive and thrive, or live and die in the repetitive and existential, futile and self-destructive, homogenized, monochromatic landscape of a brutal and bland, collective unconscious, which can spiritually result in a gradual wasting away and erosion of the senses or conflict and crisis of a desperate, disproportionate 'situational depression,' triggering and leading the narrator to feel constantly abandoned and stranded, more concretely or proverbially spoken, "the eternal stranger," where when caught between the fight or flight psychological phenomena, naturally repels him and causes him to flee and return without him even knowing it into the wild, while by sudden circumstance and coincidence discovers it surrounds the illusory-like circumference of these selfsame Monopoly board cul-de-sacs and dead ends. Most specifically, what can happen to a solitary, thoughtful, and independent thinker when being stagnated in the triangulation of a cookie-cutter, oppressive culture of a homeowner's association; A memoir all written in critical and didactic, poetic stanzas and passages, and out of desperation, when freedom and control get taken, what he is forced to do in the illusion of 'free will and volition,' something like the derivative art of a smart and ironic and social and cultural satire.

Still Time - Michael Cocchiarale

Still Time is a collection of twenty-five short and shorter stories exploring tensions that arise in a variety of contemporary relationships: a young boy must deal with the wrath of his out-of-work father; a woman runs into a man twenty years after an awkward sexual encounter; a wife, unable to conceive, imagines her own murder, as well as the reaction of her emotionally distant husband; a soon-to-be tenured English professor tries to come to terms with her husband's shocking return to the religion of his youth; an assembly line worker, married for thirty years, discovers the surprising secret life of his recently hospitalized wife. Whether a few hundred or a few thousand words, these and other stories in the collection depict characters at moments of deep crisis. Some feel powerless, overwhelmed—unable to do much to change the course of their lives. Others rise to the occasion and, for better or for worse, say or do the thing that might transform them for good. Even in stories with the most troubling of endings, there remains the possibility of redemption. For each of the characters, there is still time.

Fomite
Burlington, Vermont

Signed Confessions - *Tom Walker*
Guilt and a desperate need to repent drive the antiheroes in Tom Walker's dark (and often darkly funny) stories:
- A gullible journalist falls for the 40-year-old stripper he profiles in a magazine.
- A faithless husband abandons his family and joins a support group for lost souls.
- A merciless prosecuting attorney grapples with the suicide of his gay son.
- An aging misanthrope must make amends to five former victims.
- An egoistic naval hero is haunted by apparitions of his dead wife and a mysterious little girl.

The seven tales in *Signed Confessions* measure how far guilty men will go to obtain a forgiveness no one can grant but themselves.

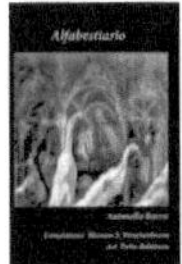 

Alfabestiario
AlphaBetaBestiario - Antonello Borra
Animals have always understood that mankind is not fully at home in the world. Bestiaries, hoping to teach, send out warnings. This one, of

Meanwell - *Janice Miller Potter*
Meanwell is a twenty-four poem sequence in which a female servant searches for identity and meaning in the shadow of her mistress, poet Anne Bradstreet. Although Meanwell herself is a fiction, someone like her could easily have existed among Bradstreet's known but unnamed domestic servants. Through Meanwell's eyes, Bradstreet emerges as a human figure during The Great Migration of the 1600s, a period in which the Massachusetts Bay Colony was fraught with physical and political dangers. Through Meanwell, the feelings of women, silenced during the midwife Anne Hutchinson's fiery trial before the Puritan ministers, are finally acknowledged. In effect, the poems are about the making of an American rebel. Through her conflicted conscience, we witness Meanwell's transformation from a powerless English waif to a mythic American who ultimately chooses wilderness over the civilization she has experienced.

Fomite
Burlington, Vermont

Love's Labours - Jack Pulaski

In the four stories and two novellas that comprise Love's Labors the protagonists Ben and Laura, discover in their fervid romance and long marriage their interlocking fates, and the histories that preceded their births. They also learned something of the paradox between love and all the things it brings to its beneficiaries: bliss, disaster, duty, tragedy, comedy, the grotesque, and tenderness.

Ben and Laura's story is also the particularly American tale of immigration to a new world. Laura's story begins in Puerto Rico, and Ben's lineage is Russian-Jewish. They meet in City College of New York, a place at least analogous to a melting pot. Laura struggles to rescue her brother from gang life and heroin. She is mother to her younger sister; their mother Consuelo is the financial mainstay of the family and consumed by work. Despite filial obligations, Laura aspires to be a serious painter. Ben writes, cares for and is caught up in the misadventures and surreal stories of his younger schizophrenic brother. Laura is also a story teller as powerful and enchanting as Scheherazade. Ben struggles to survive such riches, and he and Laura endure.

Four-Way Stop - Sherry Olson

If *Thank You* were the only prayer, as Meister Eckhart has suggested, it would be enough, and Sherry Olson's poetry, in her second book, *Four-Way Stop*, would be one. Radical attention, deep love, and dedication to kindness illuminate these poems and the stories she tells us, which are drawn from her own life: with family, with friends, and wherever she travels, with strangers – who to Olson, never are strangers, but kin.

Even at the difficult intersections, as in the title poem, *Four-Way Stop,* Olson experiences – and offers – hope, showing us how, *completely unsupervised,* people take turns, with *kindness waving each other on*. Olson writes, knowing that (to quote Czeslaw Milosz)) *What surrounds us, here and now, is not guaranteed.* To this world, with her poems, Olson brings – and teaches – attention, generosity, compassion, and appreciative joy. — Carol Henrikson

Entanglements - Tony Magistrale

A poet and a painter may employ different mediums to express the same snow-blown afternoon in January, but sometimes they find a way to capture the moment in such a way that their respective visions still manage to stir a reverberation, a connection. In part, that's what *Entanglements* seeks to do. Not so much for the poems and paintings to speak directly to one another, but for them to stir points of similarity.

Fomite
Burlington, Vermont

Did you know that you can write a review on Amazon, Good Reads or Shelfari? Just go to the book page on the website and follow the links for posting a review. Books from independent presses depend on reader to reader communications.